Fairy Tales

Imitation in Writing
Book 2

Fairy Tales

Imitation in Writing
Book 2

MATT WHITLING

Logos Press
AN IMPRINT OF CANON PRESS | MOSCOW, IDAHO

Fairy Tales is Book 2 in a growing series of *Imitation in Writing* materials designed to teach aspiring writers the art and discipline of crafting delightful prose and poetry.

Imitation in Writing Series

Published by Logos Press
The Curriculum Division of Canon Press
PO Box 8729, Moscow, Idaho 83843
800-488-2034 | www.logospressonline.com

Matt Whitling, *Fairy Tales: Imitation in Writing, Book 2*
Copyright ©2000, 2022 by Matt Whitling.
Third edition—2022, Logos Press. Second edition—2000, Logos School Materials (now Logos Press).
Some stories are adapted from Marian Edwardes's *Grimm's Household Tales* (1905), Lucy Crane's *Household Stories from the Collection of the Brothers Grimm* (1882), Edgar Taylor's *German Popular Stories* (1823), and Hans Christian Andersen's *Fairy Tales* (1835-37)

Cover design and illustration by Forrest Dickison
Interior design by Valerie Anne Bost
Printed in the United States of America. All rights reserved.

22 23 24 25 26 27 28 29 30 31   10 9 8 7 6 5 4 3 2 1

Contents

Introduction for the Teacher

Background

We are commanded in Scripture to imitate the Lord Jesus Christ. We are also commanded to imitate those brothers and sisters who through faith and patience have inherited the promises. To imitate something or someone means

- to do or try to do after the manner of; to follow the example of; to copy in action

- to make or produce a copy or representation of; to copy, reproduce

- to be, become, or make oneself like; to assume the aspect or semblance of; to simulate*

This God-sanctioned method of learning is an essential tool for educating young people. For example, how is it that we teach a child to perform simple physical skills such as throwing and catching? "Hold your hands **like this**. Step forward as you throw **like this**." Imitation. How is it that we teach a child how to form his letters correctly? "Hold your pencil **like this**. Look at **this 'a'**. Trace **this letter**. Now, you try to make an 'a' **like this one**." Imitation. How is it that we teach art? At Logos School students learn how to paint by imitating master painters of the past. "**This** is a good painting. Let's see if you can **reproduce it**." Imitation. How is it that music is taught, or reading, or math? Very often the best instruction in any of these areas necessarily includes imitation. Why, when it comes to teaching young people writing, do we educators regularly neglect this effective tool?

* James H. Murray, ed., *A New English Dictionary on Historical Principles*, vol. 5, part 1 (Oxford: OUP, 1901), s.v. "imitate."

WORD TO THE WISE

Paul tells the Corinthians to imitate him, just as he imitates Christ (1 Cor. 4:16, 11:1). This is because fathers are often examples that children imitate, and Paul tells the Corinthians that they do not have many spiritual fathers (4:15), so they should look to his example.

DEFINITION

Double Translation is an exercise where the students translate something both from Latin to English and from English to Latin.

HISTORY

Benjamin Franklin (1706–1790) was both a popular writer and one of America's Founding Fathers, serving in both the Continental Congress and the Constitutional Convention. He also wrote an autobiography.

Educators in seventeenth-century England knew the value of imitation as a tool through which they could teach style, particularly in the area of writing. The primary method of imitation in these English grammar schools was called Double Translation. In a double translation the teacher would translate a Latin work into English. The student was to copy this English translation over, paying close attention to every word and its significance. Then the student was to write down the English and Latin together, one above the other, making each language answer to the other. Afterward, the student translated the original Latin to English on his own. This was the first part of the translation. The second part took place ten days afterward when the student was given his final English translation and required to turn it back into good Latin.

Benjamin Franklin wrote of a similar exercise that he employed to educate himself a century later. When he was a young man he came across a particular piece of writing that he delighted in, *The Spectator*. *The Spectator* is a series of 555 popular essays published in 1711 and 1712. These essays were intended to improve manners and morals, raise the cultural level of the middle-class reader, and popularize serious ideas in science and philosophy. They were written well, the style was excellent, and Franklin wanted to imitate it. Here is Franklin's method of "double translation" regarding *The Spectator*:

> With that view (imitating this great work) I took some of the papers, and making short hints of the sentiments in each sentence, laid them by a few days, and then, without looking at the book, tried to complete the papers again, by expressing each hinted sentiment at length, and as fully as it had been expressed before, in any suitable words that should occur to me. Then I compared my *Spectator* with the original, discovered some of my faults, and corrected them.

But he realized that he needed a greater stock of words in order to add variety and clarity of thought to his writing.

> Therefore I took some of the tales in the *Spectator*, and turned them into verse; and, after a time, when I had pretty well forgotten the prose, turned them back again. I also sometimes jumbled my collection of hints into confusion, and after some weeks endeavored to reduce them into the best order, before I began to form the sentences and complete the subject. This was to teach me method in the arrangement of thoughts. By comparing my work with the original, I discovered many faults and corrected them; but I sometimes had the pleasure to fancy that, in particulars of small consequence, I had been fortunate enough to improve the method or the language, and this encouraged me to think that I might in time become to be a tolerable English writer, of which I was extremely ambitious.

Now the question is, "How can we employ a similar methodology?"

DEFINITIONS

Clarity in writing is the ability to express something as simply as possible so that readers can understand it.

Variety in writing is the ability to express something with different sentence patterns and styles.

Schedules

We know there are a lot of fables in this book. Don't feel that you need to do every single one in the book (although you can if you want to).

1. You might do a bi-weekly composition practice in which you do one story every other week. If you want, you can just read a fable for fun in the off-weeks without doing the assignment.

2. If you want a more relaxed pace and have other materials you want to supplement *Imitation in Writing* with, every three weeks you could read two of the fables out loud with your child and pick one of them to rewrite.

Classroom Instructions

DAY 1

1. CHOOSE A STUDENT READER: Send the fairy tale home with a student the night before you begin the assignment. He should be prepared to read the entire tale for the class the next day.

DAY 2

2. READ SILENTLY: Have the students read the tale quietly to themselves, paying close attention to the story line. When they are done, they should underline the vocabulary words in the tale. Discuss, by means of questioning, who the characters are in the tale and what took place.

3. STUDENT READS TALE: The student who was selected on Day 1 to read the tale now comes to the front of the class and reads the entire tale.

4. ORAL RETELLING: The teacher calls on individual students to retell the tale in their own words. These oral summaries should be short and to the point.

5. VOCABULARY: Call on one student for each of the vocabulary words. That student will read the sentence in which the word is found, providing context, and then define the word for the class. Occasionally the student's definition will need to be modified by the teacher so that it is an exact match with the vocabulary word in the tale. One-word definitions work well. The idea here is to provide the students with a synonym for each vocabulary word which could be substituted into the sentence without distorting the meaning. Have the students write the definition of each word on the blank provided.

6. OUTLINE THE PLOT: Initially this activity should be guided by the teacher and completed as a class. Providing

every other simple sentence or phrase for each scene is helpful for younger students. There is some room for variation in the exact wording of the sentence or phrase. The rules are that each phrase must be three words long, and they must represent a significant chronological event in that scene. From time to time the students will come up with a better phrase than the one provided in the Plot Key at the rear of this book. Use it, by all means.

7. CHARACTERS: At this point the students will list the main characters in the story and write a few descriptive words about each.

8. PASS IN ORIGINAL FAIRY TALE: Before the students begin rewriting the tale they must pass the original one in. Some students will want to read through the tale one more time to better understand what the whole thing is all about.

9. WRITE FIRST DRAFT: The students are now ready to rewrite the tale using their outline to guide them. I allow my students to change the characters and some of the incidental details of the story in their rewrites as long as the plot is identifiable. The exceptionally good writers in the class will thrive off of this opportunity to be innovative. The students who are less comfortable with writing will tend to stick to the same characters and incidental details; that is fine. All of the vocabulary words must be used correctly and underlined in the rewrite. The students should skip lines on the first draft to allow room for editing.

10. PARENTS EDIT: Students take their rewrites home on Day 2 for the parents to edit. This is most profitable when the parents sit down with the student and edit the tale together. Guidelines for editing can be sent home at the beginning of the year or communicated at a back-to-school night so that parents know what is expected. The edited first draft will be due on the morning of Day 3.

DAY 3

11. FINAL DRAFT: Time in class is provided for the students to work on the final draft. The students should not skip lines. I allow the students to draw a rubric at the beginning of their story if they like. This final draft will be due on the morning of Day 4.

DAY 4

12. GRADING: The grading sheet (page 15) should be duplicated, cut out, completed, and stapled to each student's rewrite. This will help the teacher to focus on the essential aspects of the composition as he is grading it and will provide specific feedback to the student and parents regarding which areas will need more attention in the future. As a rule, I deduct one point for each mistake per page for sentence structure, spelling, capitalization, and punctuation.

Homeschool Instructions
DAY 1

1. READ SILENTLY: Have the student read the tale quietly to himself, paying close attention to the storyline. When he is done, he should underline the vocabulary words in the tale. Discuss, by means of questioning, who the characters are in the tale and what took place.

2. STUDENT READS TALE: The student now reads the entire tale aloud.

3. ORAL RETELLING: The teacher asks the student to retell the tale in their own words. This oral summary should be short and to the point.

4. VOCABULARY: For each of the major vocabulary words, have your student read the sentence in which the word is found, providing context, and then define the word for the teacher. Occasionally the student's definition will need to be modified by the teacher so that it is an exact match with the vocabulary word in the tale. One-word definitions work well. The idea here is to provide the student with a synonym for each vocabulary word which could be substituted into the sentence without distorting the meaning. Have the student write the definition of each word on the blank provided.

5. OUTLINE THE PLOT: Initially this activity should be guided by the teacher and should be completed by the student. Providing every other simple sentence or phrase for each scene is helpful for younger students. There is some room for variation in the exact wording of the sentence or phrase. The rules are that each sentence or phrase must be three words long and represent a significant chronological event in that scene. From time to time the student will come up with a better sentence or phrase than the one provided in the Plot Key at the rear of this book. Use it, by all means.

6. CHARACTERS: At this point, the student will list the main characters in the story and write a few descriptive words about each.

7. PASS IN ORIGINAL FAIRY TALE: Before the student begins rewriting the tale they must pass the original one in. Some students will want to read through the tale one more time to better understand what the whole thing is all about.

8. WRITE FIRST DRAFT: The student is now ready to rewrite the tale using his outline as a guide. I allow my students

to change the characters and some of the incidental details of the story in their rewrites as long as the plot is identifiable. The exceptionally good writers will thrive off of this opportunity to be innovative. The students who are less comfortable with writing will tend to stick to the same characters and incidentals; that is fine. All of the vocabulary words must be used correctly and underlined in the rewrite. The student should skip lines on the first draft to allow room for editing.

DAY 2

9. EDIT: You will now edit your student's rewrite of the Fairy Tale. This is most profitable when you sit down with the student and edit the tale together. The edited first draft will be due on the morning of Day 3.

DAY 3

10. FINAL DRAFT: Have your student go over your edits to make a final draft. The student should not skip lines. I allow the students to draw a rubric at the beginning of their story if they like. This final draft will be due on the morning of Day 4.

DAY 4

11. GRADING: The grading sheet (page 15) should be duplicated, cut out, completed, and stapled to the student's rewrite. This will help you to focus on the essential aspects of the composition as you are grading it and will provide specific feedback to the student regarding which areas will need more attention in the future. As a rule, I deduct one point for each mistake per page for sentence structure, spelling, capitalization, and punctuation.

Example

The following samples will help you see what students will be reading and what work is expected of them.

ORIGINAL STORY

Story 11: The Elves and the Cobbler

by the Brothers Grimm

1. Mysterious Help

There was once a <u>cobbler</u> who worked very hard and was very honest. However, he could never earn enough to live upon, and at last all he had in the world was gone except for just enough leather to make one pair of shoes.

So he cut his leather out, all ready to make up the next day, and he went to bed, meaning to rise early in the morning to finish his work. His conscience was clear and his heart light amidst all his troubles, so he went peaceably to bed, left all his cares to Heaven, and soon fell asleep. In the morning, after he had said his prayers, he sat himself down to his work, when, to his great wonder, he saw the shoes, already made, upon the table. The good man knew not what to say or think at such an odd thing happening. He looked at the workmanship: there was not one false stitch in the whole job. It was all so neat and true that the shoes were quite a <u>masterpiece</u>.

HISTORY

This fairy tale appears in the original 1812 *Grimms' Fairy Tales* and is a folktale from Germany. Elves used to be thought of as demons or evil spirits that would cause troubles for humans, but by the time of Grimm's fairy tales they were thought of as small people who could be good or evil. The Grimm brothers describe them as dwarfs.

FAIRY TALES: IMITATION IN WRITING, BOOK 2

Section numbering guides students in outlining the fable on their worksheets.

Margin notes help explain the point of the fable or something interesting or unique about it.

Students will be asked to underline the lesson's vocabulary words in the story.

WORSHEET, PAGE 1

Students will write their name and the date on each worksheet.

Challenging words in each fable are listed. Students will identify them in the text and define them on the worksheet.

Numbers here correspond to section numbers in the fairy tale text.

WORKSHEET

Name: *Brian Kohl*

Date: *November 23, 2021*

Story 11: The Elves and the Cobbler

I. VOCABULARY

Underline the following words in the fable and define them below.

1. cobbler: *someone who makes shoes*
2. masterpiece: *something that has been made perfectly*
3. daybreak: *when the sun rises*
4. wights: *creatures or spirits*
5. pantaloons: *pants that are like tights*
6. caper: *to leap about*

II. PLOT

Write simple sentences to describe the main actions in each scene.

1. Mysterious Help
   a. *Poor cobbler makes shoes.*
   b. *Cobbler went to bed.*
   c. *New shoes appear.*
   d. *Someone buys shoes.*
   e. *They keep making shoes.*
   f. _____
   g. _____

2. The Discovery
   a. *They hide and watch.*
   b. *They discover elves.*
   c. *Elves dance and work.*
   d. *They are thankful.*
   e. *They make clothes.*
   f. *They hide and watch.*
   g. _____

FAIRY TALES: IMITATION IN WRITING, BOOK 2

WORKSHEET, PAGE 2

3. Mightily Delighted
a. *Elves find clothes.*
b. *Elves laugh and dance.*
c. *Elves leave forever.*
d. *They live happily.*

III. CHARACTERS

List the main characters and write a few descriptive words for each.

The Cobbler: works hard, honest, cheerful, poor
Customers: pay extra for good shoes
Elves: naked, work fast, happy with clothes
The Cobbler's Wife: grateful, makes clothes for elves

Students will learn to identify characters in a story by listing them on the worksheet.

IV. IMITATION

Rewrite "The Elves and the Cobbler" — first and second drafts.

- Be sure to include and underline all of the vocabulary words.
- Write three separate paragraphs, one for each scene (indent three times).

Bonus Challenge: Try using a different set of magical creatures!

The meat of the lesson comes in the rewriting of the story in the student's own words.

The Bonus Challenge provides extra inspiration for students who are ready to push themselves a little harder creatively.

STORY 11: THE ELVES AND THE COBBLER

STORY SHEET

Students will write their name and the date on each story sheet.

STORY SHEET

Name: _Brian Kohl_

Date: _November 23, 2021_

Title: _The Germs and the Rats_

Students must title their story. If they follow the bonus challenge, their title may not match the original.

The first line should be indented.

Once, not so very long ago, there lived some rats. They were professionals at candle making. The only things they didn't like about candle making were they couldn't do their work openly because they lived in a cobbler's house and the cobbler hated rats. They also didn't like having to dip their paws into the hot wax when a string fell into it. Slowly their business went down hill and finally they only had enough wax to make one more spice candle. The husband got out the wax and started the oven to melt it. Next he and his wife went to bed. At daybreak he came down to start working. He saw before him a masterpiece candle: it had no bumps and the string was right in the middle. Mrs. Bump (a frog) came in and snatched the candle up and gave him 25 shillings (by the way, the candle was only 10 shillings) and walked out with the candle. The rat bought 12 wax wads for 12 new candles. This went on for some time. What ratty put out was done by morning.

All vocabulary words should be included and underlined.

One day Mr. Rat said, "Why not find out who gives us this fortune?" She said, "All right." So they stayed up and around midnight in ran fifty little germs. The little wights without any pantaloons began to caper

AESOP'S FABLES: IMITATION IN WRITING, BOOK 1

A blank second page lets students spill over to the back if their story doesn't fit on the front.

A blank, reproducible story sheet appears on page 13.

STORY SHEET

Name: _____

Date: _____

Title: _____

_____

_____

_____

_____

_____

_____

_____

_____

_____

_____

_____

_____

_____

_____

_____

_____

_____

_____

_____

_____

_____

_____

_____

_____

GRADING SHEET

Student: _____

Story #: _____

Plot Outline   _____/10

Handwriting   _____/10

Title/Indent   _____/5

Vocabulary Usage   _____/15

Sentence Structure   _____/15

Spelling/Punctuation/

    Capitalization   _____/25

Storyline   _____/20

TOTAL   _____/100

GRADING SHEET

Student: _____

Story #: _____

Plot Outline   _____/10

Handwriting   _____/10

Title/Indent   _____/5

Vocabulary Usage   _____/15

Sentence Structure   _____/15

Spelling/Punctuation/

    Capitalization   _____/25

Storyline   _____/20

TOTAL   _____/100

GRADING SHEET

Student: _____

Story #: _____

Plot Outline   _____/10

Handwriting   _____/10

Title/Indent   _____/5

Vocabulary Usage   _____/15

Sentence Structure   _____/15

Spelling/Punctuation/

    Capitalization   _____/25

Storyline   _____/20

TOTAL   _____/100

GRADING SHEET

Student: _____

Story #: _____

Plot Outline   _____/10

Handwriting   _____/10

Title/Indent   _____/5

Vocabulary Usage   _____/15

Sentence Structure   _____/15

Spelling/Punctuation/

    Capitalization   _____/25

Storyline   _____/20

TOTAL   _____/100

Story 1:
Why the Bear Has a Stumpy Tail

by George Webbe Dasent

1. Slinking Along

One winter's day the bear met the fox, who came slinking along with a string of fish he had stolen.

"Hey, wait a minute! Where did you get those fish?" demanded the bear.

"Oh, my Lord Bruin, I've been out fishing and caught them," said the fox. So the bear was going to learn to fish, too, and bade the fox to tell him how he was to set about it.

2. Bad Advice

"Oh, it is quite easy," answered the fox, "and soon learned. You've only got to go upon the ice, and cut a hole and stick your tail down through it. Hold it there as long as you can. Don't worry if it smarts a little; that's when the fish bite. The longer you hold it there, the more fish you'll get. Then all at once, yank your tail out with a cross-pull sideways and a strong pull, too."

HISTORY

This story is a Norwegian folk tale that was first published in 1874. It is very similar to Rudyard Kipling's *Just So Stories.*

3. A Strong Pull

Well, the bear did as the fox said, and though he felt very cold and his tail smarted very much, he kept it a long, long time down in the hole, till at last it was frozen in, though of course he did not know that. Then he pulled it out with a strong pull, and it snapped short off, and that's why bruin goes about with a stumpy tail to this day!

FINIS

WORKSHEET

Story 1: Why the Bear Has a Stumpy Tail

I. VOCABULARY

Underline the following words in the fable and define them below:

1. slinking _____

2. demanded _____

3. bruin _____

4. bade _____

5. smarts _____

6. stumpy _____

II. PLOT

Write simple sentences to describe the main actions in each scene. Sample answers are given for the first scene.

1. Slinking Along

a. *Bear meets fox.*

b. *Fox has fish.*

c. *Bear asks advice.*

2. Bad Advice

a. _____

b. _____

c. _____

d. _____

3. A Strong Pull

a. _____

b. _____

c. _____

d. _____

e. _____

III. CHARACTERS

List the main characters and write a few descriptive words for each:

_____

_____

_____

_____

_____

_____

IV. IMITATION

Rewrite "Why the Bear Has a Stumpy Tail" using only your outline (no looking back at the original story). Write a first draft on blank paper, then write a final draft on a story sheet.

- Be sure to include and underline all of the vocabulary words.
- Write three separate paragraphs, one for each scene (indent three times).

Bonus Challenge: Write about how some other animal became the way it is. For instance, how did the flamingo become pink? Where did the platypus get its fur or bill?

Story 2:
The Princess and the Pea

by Hans Christian Andersen

1. The Search

Once upon a time there was a prince who wanted to marry a princess, but he wanted to make very sure he only married a real princess. He traveled all over the world to find one, but nowhere could he get what he wanted. There were princesses enough, but it was difficult to find out whether they were real ones.

There was always something about them that was not as it should be. So he came home again and was despondent, for he would have liked very much to have a real princess.

2. The Test

One evening a terrible storm came on; there was thunder and lightning, and the rain poured down in torrents. Suddenly a knocking was heard at the city gate, and the old king went to open it.

It was a princess standing out there in front of the gate. But, good gracious! what a sight the rain and the wind had made her look. The water ran down from her hair and clothes; it ran down into

HISTORY

"The Princess and the Pea" was first published by Hans Christian Andersen in 1835. It came from either Denmark or Sweden, and it is a great example of how you can tell who the true queen is.

the toes of her shoes and out again at the heels. And yet she said that she was a real princess.

"Well, we'll soon find that out," thought the old queen. But she said nothing, went into the bedroom, took all the bedding off the bedstead, and laid a pea on the bottom. Then she took twenty mattresses and laid them on the pea, and then put twenty eiderdown beds on top of the mattresses.

On this the princess had to lie all night. In the morning they asked her how she had slept.

3. The Outcome

"Oh, very badly!" said she. "I have scarcely closed my eyes all night. Heaven only knows what was in the bed, but I was lying on something hard. I am black and blue all over my body. It is quite dreadful!"

Now they knew that she was a real princess because she had felt the pea right through the twenty mattresses and the twenty eiderdown beds. Nobody but a real princess could be as sensitive as that.

So the prince took her for his wife, for now he knew that he had a real princess; and the pea was put in the museum, where it may still be seen, if no one has stolen it.

FINIS

Name: _____

Date: _____

Story 2: The Princess and the Pea

I. VOCABULARY

Underline the following words in the fable, and define them below.

1. torrents: _____

2. bedstead: _____

3. eider: _____

4. scarcely: _____

5. dreadful: _____

6. sensitive: _____

II. PLOT

Write simple sentences to describe the main actions in each scene.

1. The Search

a. _____

b. _____

c. _____

d. _____

2. The Test

a. _____

b. _____

c. _____

d. _____

3. The Outcome

a. _____

b. _____

c. _____

d. _____

e. _____

III. CHARACTERS

List the main characters and write a few descriptive words for each.

_____

_____

_____

_____

_____

_____

IV. IMITATION

Rewrite "The Princess and the Pea" using only your outline (no looking back at the original story). Write a first draft on blank paper, then write a final draft on a story sheet.

- Be sure to include and underline all of the vocabulary words.

- Write three separate paragraphs, one for each scene (indent three times).

Bonus Challenge: Make the test something different, just so long as the princess's sensitivity is still miraculously great!

Story 3:
The Fox and the Horse

by the Brothers Grimm

1. Turned Adrift

A farmer had a horse that had been an excellent faithful servant to him; but he was now grown too old to work, so the farmer would give him nothing more to eat. He said, "I don't want you anymore, so get out of my stable. I shall not take you back again until you are stronger than a lion." Then he opened the door and turned him adrift.

The poor horse was very melancholy and wandered up and down in the wood, seeking some little shelter from the cold wind and rain. Presently a fox met him. "What's the matter, my friend?" said he. "Why do you hang down your head and look so lonely and sad?"

"Ah!" replied the horse, "justice and avarice never dwell in the same house. My master has forgotten all that I have done for him so many years, and because I can no longer work, he has turned me adrift. He says unless I become stronger than a lion, he will not take me back

HISTORY

"The Fox and the Horse" is another Grimm story. You might find it familiar to the story of Charlotte's Web, where an animal that is turned out and left to die proves its worth through a clever trick.

again. What chance do I have of that? He knows I have none, or he would not talk so."

2. The Plan

However, the fox bade him be of good cheer and said: "I will help you. Lie down there; stretch yourself out quite stiff, and pretend to be dead."

The horse did as he was told, and the fox went straight to the lion who lived in a cave close by, and said to him: "A little way off lies a dead horse. Come with me and you may make an excellent meal of his carcass."

The lion was greatly pleased and set off immediately; and when they came to the horse, the fox said: "You will not be able to eat him comfortably here. I'll tell you what—I will tie you fast to his tail, and then you can draw him to your den and eat him at your leisure."

3. Hog-tied

This advice pleased the lion, so he laid himself down quietly for the fox to make him fast to the horse. But the fox managed to tie the lion's legs together and bound all so hard and fast that with all his strength he could not set himself free. When the work was done, the fox clapped the horse on the shoulder and said: "Giddyup, dobbin! Giddyup!" Then up he sprang and moved off, dragging the lion behind him. The beast began to roar and bellow, till all the birds of the wood flew away for fright; but the horse let him sing on and made his way quietly over the fields to his master's house.

"Here he is, master," said he. "I have got the better of him."

When the farmer saw his old servant, his heart relented, and he said, "You will stay in your stable and be well taken care of." And so the poor old horse had plenty to eat and lived—till he died.

FINIS

Story 3: The Fox and the Horse

V. VOCABULARY

Underline the following words in the fable and define them below.

1. adrift: _____

2. melancholy: _____

3. justice: _____

4. avarice: _____

5. carcass: _____

6. relented: _____

VI. PLOT

Write simple sentences to describe the main actions in each scene.

1. Turned Adrift   2. The Plan

a. _____   a. _____

b. _____   b. _____

c. _____   c. _____

d. _____   d. _____

e. _____

f. _____

3. Hog-tied

a. _____

b. _____

c. _____

d. _____

e. _____

f. _____

VII. CHARACTERS

List the main characters and write a few descriptive words for each.

_____

_____

_____

_____

_____

_____

VIII. IMITATION

Rewrite "The Fox and the Horse" using only your outline (no looking back at the original story). Write a first draft on blank paper, then write a final draft on a story sheet.

- Be sure to include and underline all of the vocabulary words.

- Write three separate paragraphs, one for each scene (indent three times).

Bonus Challenge: Retell the story with a different set of animals.

Story 4:
Ali and the Sultan's Saddle

from The Arabian Nights

1. Ali's Jokes

Once upon a time there lived a very powerful Sultan whose kingdom stretched to the edges of the desert. One of his subjects was called Ali, a man who enjoyed making fun of his ruler. He invented all sorts of tales about the Sultan and his Court, and folk would roar with laughter at his jokes. Indeed, Ali became so well-known, that people pointed him out in the street and chuckled.

Ali's fun at the Sultan's expense reached the point where the Sultan himself heard about it. Angry and insulted, he ordered the guards to bring the joker before him.

"I shall punish him for his cheek," said the Sultan eagerly, as he rubbed his hands, thinking of the good whipping he was about to administer.

2. Before the Sultan

But when Ali was brought before him, he bowed so low that his forehead scraped the floor.

HISTORY

The Arabian Nights is a collection of stories that was written as early as the ninth century AD, but it was first translated into English in 1775 as *One Thousand and One Nights*. The whole story is framed by the tale of a sultan who would marry lady after lady and then kill her the next day! Finally, one girl married him, but told such good stories with such exciting cliff-hangers that he kept sparing her for a thousand nights until he finally decided to spare her life.

Giving the Sultan no time to open his mouth, Ali said; "Sire! Please let me thank you for granting my dearest wish: to look upon you in person and tell you how greatly I admire your wisdom and handsome figure. I've written a poem about you. May I recite it to you?"

Overwhelmed by this stream of words and delighted at Ali's unexpected praise, the Sultan told him to recite his poem. In actual fact, Ali hadn't written a single word, so he had to invent it as he went along, and this he did, loudly comparing the Sultan's splendor to that of the sun, his strength to that of the tempest, and his voice to the sound of the wind. Everyone applauded and cheered. Now quite charmed, the Sultan forgot why he had called Ali before him and clapped at the end of the poem in his honor.

3. Ali's Reward

"Well done!" he cried. "You're a fine poet and deserve a reward. Choose one of these saddles as payment for your ability." Ali picked up a donkey's saddle and, thanking the Sultan, he hurried out of the palace with the saddle on his back. When people saw him rush along, they all asked him, "Ali, where are you going with that donkey's saddle on your back?"

"I've just recited a poem in honor of the Sultan, and he's given me one of his own robes as a reward!"

And winking Ali pointed to the saddle!

FINIS

Name: _____

Date: _____

Story 4: Ali and the Sultan's Saddle

I. VOCABULARY

Underline the following words in the fable and define them below.

1. subjects: _____

2. Sultan: _____

3. insulted: _____

4. cheek: _____

5. recite: _____

6. applauded: _____

II. PLOT

Write simple sentences to describe the main actions in each scene.

1. Ali's Jokes

a. _____

b. _____

c. _____

d. _____

2. Before the Sultan

a. _____

b. _____

c. _____

d. _____

e. _____

f. _____

g. _____

h. _____

3. Ali's reward

a. _____

b. _____

c. _____

d. _____

e. _____

f. _____

g. _____

III. BIBLE VERSES

Copy out these verses from your Bible, and think about how they relate to the story:

1. Exodus 22:28: _____

_____

_____

2. Acts 23:5: _____

_____

_____

_____

IV. IMITATION

Rewrite "Ali and the Sultan's Saddle"—first and second drafts.

- Include and underline all the vocabulary words in your rewrite.

- Write three separate paragraphs, one for each scene (indent three times).

Bonus Challenge: Pick something different than a saddle. Make sure it's exotic!

Story 5:
The Straw, the Coal, and the Bean

by the Brothers Grimm

1. Great Escape

There lived in a certain village a poor old woman who had collected a mess of beans and was going to cook them. So she made a fire on her hearth, and, in order to make it burn better, she put in a handful of straw. When the beans began to bubble in the pot, one of them fell out and lay, never noticed, near a piece of straw which was already there. Soon a red-hot coal jumped out of the fire and joined the pair. The straw began first and said, "Dear friends, how did you end up here?"

The coal answered, "I jumped out of the fire by great good luck, or I should certainly have met my death. I should have been burned to ashes."

The bean said, "I too have come out of it with a whole skin. If the old woman had kept me in the pot, I should have been cooked into a soft mass like my comrades."

"Nor should I have met with a better fate," said the straw; "the old woman has turned my brothers into fire and smoke, sixty of them she

HISTORY

This is another story from the Brothers Grimm. It is half a just-so story, which reminds us of how disastrous leaving a job half-done can be. The coal stops in the river, and his fear is what leads to him and the straw getting destroyed.

took up at once and deprived of life. Very lucki-ly I managed to slip through her fingers."

2. Joined in Fellowship

"What should we do now?" said the coal.

"I think," answered the bean, "that as we have been so lucky as to escape with our lives, we should join together, and, lest any more bad fortune might happen to us here, we should go abroad into foreign lands."

The proposal pleased the two others, and forthwith they started on their travels. Soon they came to a little brook, and as there was no stepping-stone and no bridge, they could not tell how they were to get to the other side. The straw was struck with a good idea and said, "I will lay myself across, so that you can go over me as if I were a bridge!"

3. Black Seam

So the straw stretched himself from one bank to the other, and the coal, who was of an ardent nature, quickly trotted up to go over the newly made bridge. When, however, she reached the middle and heard the water rushing past beneath her, she was struck with terror and stopped and could get no farther. So the straw began to get burnt, broke in two pieces, and fell in the brook, and the coal slipped down, hissing as she touched the water, and melted into nothing. The bean, who had prudently remained behind on the bank, could not help laughing at the sight and, not being able to contain herself, went on laughing so excessively that she burst. And she certainly would have been undone forever if a tailor on his travels had not by good luck stopped to rest himself by the brook. As he had a compassionate heart, he took out needle and thread and stitched her together again. The bean thanked him in the most elegant manner, but as he had sewn her up with black stitches, all beans since then have a black seam.

FINIS

WORSHEET

Story 5: The Straw, the Coal, and the Bean

I. VOCABULARY

Underline the following words in the fable and define them below.

1. comrades: _____

2. foreign: _____

3. proposal: _____

4. forthwith: _____

5. brook: _____

6. ardent: _____

II. PLOT

Write simple sentences to describe the main actions in each scene.

1. Great Escape

a. _____

b. _____

c. _____

d. _____

e. _____

2. Joined in Fellowship

a. _____

b. _____

c. _____

3. Black Seam

a. _____

b. _____

c. _____

d. _____

e. _____

f. _____

g. _____

III. CHARACTERS

List the main characters and write a few descriptive words for each.

_____

_____

_____

_____

_____

_____

IV. IMITATION

Rewrite "The Straw, the Coal, and the Bean"—first and final drafts.

- Be sure to include and underline all of the vocabulary words.
- Write three separate paragraphs, one for each scene (indent three times).

Bonus Challenge: Pick a different set of plants or vegetables to go across the stream, only making sure that one of them survives with some sort of mark, like the bean's seam in the story.

Story 6:
The Three Billy Goats Gruff

Retold from *East of the Sun and West of the Moon*

1. Greener Grass

Once there were three billy goats who lived together, and the name of all three was "Gruff." One day the big billy goat said to the others, "Let us go across the bridge to the hillside to make ourselves fat. You be the first to go, little billy goat." Now under the bridge that they had to cross lived a great ugly troll whose eyes were as big as saucers and whose nose was as long as a poker.

2. Two Across

The littlest billy goat Gruff started boldly across the bridge. "Trip-trap; trip-trap!" went his hoofs on the bridge. When he had reached the middle of the bridge, the old troll roared, "Who is that trip-trapping on my bridge?"

"Oh it is only I, the little billy goat Gruff. I am going over to the hillside to make myself fat," replied the goat in a small voice.

"Don't you go any farther for I am coming up to gobble you up," replied the troll.

HISTORY

This is another Norwegian fairy tale from the same collection as "The Bear with the Stumpy Tail." It features the remarkable creatures called Trolls, who went far back to the Norse mythology of the Prose Edda. They lived in mountains, rocks, and caves, much as this troll lives under a bridge.

"Oh don't eat me," said the goat. "Wait for the second billy goat Gruff. He is much bigger than I am."

"All right—off you go," said the troll. "Since I am pretty hungry today, I shall wait for your brother."

So the little billy goat Gruff went over the bridge and was soon munching on the tender green grass.

Next came the middle billy goat Gruff. He was fatter than the first and his feet went, "TRIP-TRAP; TRIP-TRAP!" on the bridge. When he had reached the middle of the bridge, the troll roared, "*Who goes trip-trapping over my bridge?*"

"It is I, the middle billy goat Gruff. I am going over the bridge to the hillside to make myself fat," replied the middle billy goat in a strong voice.

"Don't you go any farther," roared the troll, "for I am coming to eat you up."

"Please do not eat me up. Wait for the big billy goat Gruff. He is much fatter than I am," said the middle billy goat Gruff.

"Very well," said the troll. "I am pretty hungry today so I shall wait. Off you go." So the middle billy goat went across the bridge and was soon eating the green grass with his brother.

3. Butted off

Now the great big billy goat Gruff started across the bridge. He was so fat and heavy that his feet went, "TRIP-TRAP; TRIP-TRAP," and the bridge groaned and swayed under his weight.

"*Who is that trip-trapping over my bridge?*" roared the troll.

In a strong voice the big billy goat answered, "It is I! The big billy goat Gruff!"

"Well, I am coming to gobble you up," roared the troll.

Then the big billy goat answered:

> "Well come, I have two horns so strong
>   and stout,
> With them I'll poke your eyeballs out.
> I have four hoofs as hard as stones,
> With them I'll break your body and
>   bones."

With that he flew at the troll and butted him into the river. That was the last that was ever heard of the troll. After that the big billy goat went up to the hillside and joined his brothers. There they got so fat that they were hardly able to walk home again. And if they haven't gotten thinner, why they're still fat; and so,

Snip, snap, snout,
This tale's told out.

FINIS

WORKSHEET

Name: _____

Date: _____

Story 6: The Three Billy Goats Gruff

I. VOCABULARY

Underline the following words in the fable and define them below.

1. troll: _____

2. boldly: _____

3. roared: _____

4. swayed: _____

5. stout: _____

6. butted: _____

II. PLOT

Write simple sentences to describe the main actions in each scene.

1. Greener Grass

a. _____

b. _____

c. _____

d. _____

e. _____

2. Two Across

a. _____

b. _____

c. _____

d. _____

e. _____

f. _____

3. Butted Off

a. _____

b. _____

c. _____

d. _____

III. CHARACTERS

List the main characters and write a few descriptive words for each.

_____

_____

_____

_____

_____

_____

IV. IMITATION

Rewrite "The Three Billy Goats Gruff"—first and second drafts.

- Be sure to include and underline all of the vocabulary words.
- Write three separate paragraphs, one for each scene (indent three times).

Bonus Challenge: See if you can put this fairy tale into the real world, with real people and a real (non-magical) danger.

Story 7:
The Pied Piper of Hamelin

by the Brothers Grimm

1. Rats in Hamelin

Many years ago in Germany in the town of Hamelin there were rats, rats, rats. The town was very pretty. There were trees along the streets and not far away was a beautiful river. But all the beauty of the town was spoiled by so many rats. They were in the streets and in the houses. They were into everything and the people had no peace. At last they went to the Mayor and told him that he must get rid of the rats. The Mayor did not know of any way to rid the town of the rats. He thought and thought but he could not think of a plan.

2. Strange Piper

Just then there was a tap at the door and the Mayor called, "Come in." And in came a stranger. He was a very queer looking fellow—half of his coat was yellow, and half was red. He was tall and thin, and each blue eye was sharp like a pin. Around his neck hung a flute.

HISTORY

The story of the pied piper goes back to the Middle Ages. It was eventually re-written as a poem by Johann Wolfgang von Goethe in 1803, and the Brothers Grimm included it in another of their folklore collections.

"Good Day," said the stranger. "I hear you are troubled with rats in this town. Would you like to be rid of them?"

"Indeed we would," replied the Mayor. "But who are you and how do I know that you can rid the town of rats?"

"I am the Pied Piper," said he. "I can play on my flute, music that will charm all things under the sun. Will you give me a thousand guilders to take all the rats away from here?"

"Agreed," said the Mayor.

The Piper went out into the street and put his flute up to his mouth. Up one street and down another he went, playing a mysterious tune. Soon a strange thing happened. Tiny squeaks began to be heard and they grew louder and louder and out of the houses the rats came trembling; all kinds of rats—little rats, big rats, lean rats, fat rats, brown rats, black rats, white rats, gray rats. Every rat in the town followed him as he played his music. He led them on until he came to the river and because they wanted to get nearer to the wonderful music, they did not see where they were going. They all fell into the river, and every one was drowned.

3. A Different Tune

The Piper returned to the Mayor for the thousand guilders but the Mayor said, "Surely you know that I was only joking."

"But I was not joking," said the Piper, "Will you give me the money or not?"

Still the Mayor refused and in parting the Piper said, "You'll be sorry for I have another tune to play for people who do not keep their word."

He went into the street once more and began to play on the flute. This time the music was rollicking and soon out of the houses the children came running. They danced and sang and followed the Piper wherever he went. It seemed that they could not help themselves. He led them around the streets and then led them away from the town. The parents called and called, but the children didn't heed them.

The Piper led them to a mountain and when they reached it a door in the side of the mountain opened and in went the Piper and all the children. That was the last the people of Hamelin ever saw of the Piper or the children. And oh, how lonesome it was in the town with all the children gone.

FINIS

WORKSHEET

Name: _____

Date: _____

Story 7: The Pied Piper of Hamelin

I. VOCABULARY

Underline the following words in the fable and define them below.

1. spoiled: _____

2. queer: _____

3. guilders: _____

4. mysterious: _____

5. rollicking: _____

6. heed: _____

II. PLOT

Write simple sentences to describe the main actions in each scene.

1. Rats in Hamelin

a. _____

b. _____

c. _____

2. Strange Piper

a. _____

b. _____

c. _____

d. _____

e. _____

3. A Different Tune

a. _____

b. _____

c. _____

d. _____

e. _____

III. CHARACTERS

List the main characters and write a few descriptive words for each.

_____

_____

_____

_____

_____

_____

IV. IMITATION

Rewrite "The Pied Piper of Hamelin"—first and second drafts.

- Be sure to include and underline all of the vocabulary words.
- Write three separate paragraphs, one for each scene (indent three times).

Bonus Challenge: Have the pied piper use some other magical means of attracting the rats and the children.

Story 8:
The Queen Bee

by the Brothers Grimm

1. Mercy Shown

Once upon a time, the king's sons went out into the world to seek their fortunes; but they soon fell into a wasteful, foolish way of living, so that they could not return home again. Then their young brother, who was a little insignificant dwarf, went out to seek his brothers. When he had found them, they only laughed at him to think that he, who was so young and simple, should try to travel through the world, when they who were so much wiser had been unable to make their way in it.

However, they all set out on their journey together and came at last to an anthill. The two elder brothers would have pulled it down, in order to see how the poor ants in their fright would run about and carry off their eggs. But the little dwarf said, "Let the poor things enjoy themselves; I will not let you trouble them."

So on they went and came to a lake where many, many ducks were swimming about. The two brothers wanted to catch two and roast

HISTORY

Here is another story of the Brothers Grimm, and it is also very similar to "The Three Little Pigs." In both stories, it is the youngest, most enterprising brother who saves his older foolish brothers. It is also a good example of a story with three tasks, with the last one being the most difficult.

them. But the dwarf said, "Let the poor things enjoy themselves; you shall not kill them."

Next they came to a bees nest in a hollow tree, and there was so much honey that it ran down the trunk, and the two brothers wanted to light a fire under the tree and kill the bees to get their honey. But the dwarf held them back and said, "Let the pretty insects enjoy themselves; I cannot let you burn them."

2. A Thousand Pearls

After a while, the three brothers came to a castle. As they passed by the stables, they saw fine horses standing there, but all were made of marble, and no man was to be seen. Then they went through all the rooms till they came to a door which had three locks. In the middle of the door was a wicket, so that they could look into the next room. There they saw a little gray old man sitting at a table. They called to him once or twice, but he did not hear. However, they called a third time, and then he rose and came out to them.

He said nothing but took hold of them and led them to a beautiful table covered with all sorts of good things; and when they had eaten and drunk he showed each of them to a bedchamber.

The next morning he came to the eldest and took him to a marble table, where were three tablets which described how the castle might be disenchanted. The first tablet said, "In the wood, under the moss, lie a thousand pearls belonging to the king's daughter. They must all be found. If one is missing at sunset, he who seeks them will be turned into marble."

The eldest brother set out and sought for the pearls the whole day. But the evening came, and he had only found the first hundred, so he was turned into stone as the tablet had foretold.

The next day, the second brother undertook the task. He succeeded no better than the first, for he could only find the second hundred of the pearls, and therefore he, too, was turned into stone.

3. The Disenchantment

At last came the little dwarf's turn. He looked in the moss, but it was so hard to find the pearls, and the job was so tiresome that he sat down upon a stone and cried. And as he sat there the king of the ants (whose life he had saved) came to help him with five thousand ants. It was not long before they had found all the pearls and laid them in a heap.

The second tablet said, "The key of the princess's bedchamber must be fished up out of the lake." As the dwarf came to the brink of it, he saw the ducks whose lives he had saved swimming about. They dived down and soon brought up the key from the bottom.

The third task was the hardest. It was to choose out the youngest and the best of the king's three daughters. Now they were all beautiful and all exactly alike; but he was told that the eldest had eaten a piece of sugar, the next some sweet syrup, and the youngest a spoonful of honey. So he was to guess which it was that had eaten the honey.

Then came the queen of the bees, who had been saved by the little dwarf from the fire, and she tried the lips of all three. At last, she sat upon the lips of the one that had eaten the honey; and so the dwarf knew which was the youngest. Thus the spell was broken, and all who had been turned into stones awoke and took their proper forms. The dwarf's two older brothers married the two older sisters, but the dwarf himself married the youngest and the best of the princesses and was king after her father's death.

FINIS

WORKSHEET

Name: _____

Date: _____

Story 8: The Queen Bee

I. VOCABULARY

Underline the following words in the fable and define them below.

1. insignificant: _____

2. dwarf: _____

3. wicket: _____

4. chamber: _____

5. disenchanted: _____

6. proper: _____

II. PLOT

Write simple sentences to describe the main actions in each scene.

1. Mercy Shown

a. _____

b. _____

c. _____

d. _____

e. _____

2. A Thousand Pearls

a. _____

b. _____

c. _____

d. _____

e. _____

f. _____

3. The Disenchantment

a. _____

b. _____

c. _____

d. _____

e. _____

f. _____

g. _____

III. CHARACTERS

List the main characters and write a few descriptive words for each.

_____

_____

_____

_____

_____

_____

IV. IMITATION

Rewrite "The Queen Bee"—first and second drafts.

- Be sure to include and underline all of the vocabulary words.

- Write three separate paragraphs, one for each scene (indent three times).

Bonus Challenge: Change the tasks and the animals, and see what you come up with.

Story 9: Old Sultan

by the Brothers Grimm

1. Useless

A shepherd had a faithful dog, called Sultan, who had grown very old and lost all his teeth. One day when the shepherd and his wife were standing together before the house, the shepherd said, "I will shoot old Sultan tomorrow morning, for he is of no use now."

But his wife said: "Pray let the poor creature live; he has served us well a great many years, and we ought to give him a livelihood for the rest of his days."

"But what can we do with him?" said the shepherd. "He has not a tooth in his head, and the thieves don't care for him at all. It's true, he has served us, but he did it to earn his livelihood. Tomorrow shall be his last day."

2. The Rescue

Poor Sultan, who was lying close by them, heard all that the shepherd and his wife said to each other and was very much frightened to think

HISTORY

This is just like "The Horse and the Fox": an old animal is going to be abandoned, but he redeems himself in the eyes of his owner at the last moment.

tomorrow would be his last day. So in the evening, he went to his good friend the wolf, who lived in the wood, and told him all his sorrows and how his master meant to kill him in the morning.

"Do not worry," said the wolf. "I will give you some good advice. Your master, you know, goes out every morning very early with his wife into the field, and they take their little child with them and lay it down behind the hedge in the shade while they are at work. Lie down close by the child, and pretend to be watching it, and I will come out of the wood and run away with it. You must run after me as fast as you can, and I will let it drop. Then you can carry it back, and they will think you have saved their child and will be so thankful to you that they will take care of you as long as you live."

The dog liked this plan very well, and so he carried it out. The wolf ran with the child a little way. The shepherd and his wife screamed out, but Sultan soon overtook him and carried the poor little thing back to his master and mistress. Then the shepherd patted him on the head and said, "Old Sultan has saved our child from the wolf! He shall live and be well taken care of and have plenty to eat. Wife, go home and give him a good dinner, and let him have my old cushion to sleep on as long as he lives."

3. One Good Turn . . .

Soon afterward the wolf came and wished him joy and said, "Now, my good fellow, you must tell no tales, but turn your head the other way when I want to taste one of the old shepherd's fine fat sheep."

"No," said Sultan; "I will be true to my master."

However, the wolf thought he was joking and came one night to get a dainty morsel. But Sultan had told his master what the wolf meant to do, so the shepherd lay in wait for him behind the barn door. When the wolf was busy looking for a good fat sheep, his back was struck with stout cudgel.

Then the wolf was very angry and called Sultan an old rogue and swore he would have his revenge. So the next morning the wolf sent the boar to challenge Sultan to come into the wood to fight him. Now Sultan had nobody he could ask to be his second in the duel besides the shepherd's old three-legged cat. So he took her with him, and as the poor thing limped along with some trouble, she stuck up her tail straight in the air.

The wolf and the wild boar were first on the scene. When they spied their enemies coming and saw the cat's long tail standing straight in the air, they thought she was carrying a sword for Sultan to fight with; and every time she limped, they thought she was picking up a stone to throw at them. They said they did not like this way of fighting, and the boar lay down behind a bush, and the wolf jumped up into a tree. Sultan and the cat soon came up and looked about and were amazed that no one was there.

The boar, however, had not quite hidden himself, for his ears stuck out of the bush. When he shook one of them a little, the cat, seeing something move and thinking it was a mouse, sprang for it. She bit and scratched the boar so terribly that he jumped up and grunted and ran away, roaring out, "Look up in the tree—there sits the one who is to blame." So they looked up and saw the wolf sitting among the branches. They called him a cowardly rascal and would not let him come down till he was heartily ashamed of himself and promised to be good friends again with old Sultan.

FINIS

WORKSHEET

Name: _____

Date: _____

Story 9: Old Sultan

I. VOCABULARY

Underline the following words in the fable and define them below.

1. pray: _____

2. livelihood: _____

3. overtook: _____

4. dainty: _____

5. cudgel: _____

6. ashamed: _____

II. PLOT

Write simple sentences to describe the main actions in each scene.

1. Useless

a. _____

b. _____

c. _____

d. _____

e. _____

2. The Rescue

a. _____

b. _____

c. _____

d. _____

3. One Good Turn . . .

a. _____

b. _____

c. _____

d. _____

e. _____

f. _____

g. _____

III. CHARACTERS

List the main characters and write a few descriptive words for each.

_____

_____

_____

_____

_____

_____

IV. IMITATION

Rewrite "Old Sultan"—first and second drafts.

- Be sure to include and underline all of the vocabulary words.

- Write three separate paragraphs, one for each scene (indent three times).

Bonus Challenge: Include humans in your version, and see if you can make it more exciting. Replace the cat with something funny. For example, maybe some bandits mistake an old woman for the sheriff.

Story 10:
The Mouse, the Bird, and the Sausage

by the Brothers Grimm

1. FOWL DISCONTENT

Once upon a time, a mouse, a bird, and a sausage entered into partnership and set up house together. For a long time all went well. The three of them lived in great comfort and added a lot to their stores. The bird's duty was to fly daily into the wood and bring in the fuel; the mouse fetched the water, and the sausage saw to the cooking.

When people are too well off, they always begin to long for something new. And so it came to pass that the bird, while out one day, met a fellow-bird, to whom he boasted about the excellence of his household arrangements. But the other bird sneered at him for being a poor fool. He said, "You do all the hard work, while the other two stay at home and get to take advantage of you." For the bird had told him that after the mouse had made the fire and fetched in the water, she could just go into her little room and rest until it was time to set the table. The sausage had only to watch the pot to see that the food

HISTORY

This is a fun story about what happens when people switch roles just because they are tired of what they are doing right now. The grass is always greener on the other side.

was properly cooked, and when it was near dinnertime he just threw himself into the broth or rolled in and out among the vegetables three or four times, then the vegetables would be buttered and salted and ready to be served. Then, when the bird himself came home and had laid aside his burden, they all sat down at the table, and when they had finished their meal, they could sleep their fill till the following morning. It was a really delightful life.

2. CONTENT CANINE

After his friend had made fun of him for being taken advantage of, the bird next morning refused to bring in the wood, telling the others that he had been their servant long enough and had been a fool in the bargain. He wanted to make a change and to try some other way of arranging the work. Beg and pray as the mouse and the sausage might, it was of no use; the bird remained master of the situation, and they had to try his idea. They therefore drew lots, and it fell to the sausage to bring in the wood, to the mouse to cook, and to the bird to fetch the water.

And now what happened? The sausage went off in search of wood, the bird made the fire, and the mouse put on the pot, and then these two waited till the sausage returned with the fuel for the following day. But the sausage remained so long away that they became uneasy and the bird flew out to meet him. He had not flown far, however, when he came across a dog who, having met the sausage, had regarded him as his legitimate booty, and had seized and swallowed him.

The bird complained to the dog of this barefaced robbery, but nothing he said was of any avail. The dog answered that he had found false credentials on the sausage, and that was the reason he had eaten him. The bird picked up the wood and flew sadly home and told the mouse all he had seen and heard. They were both very unhappy but agreed to make the best of things and to remain with each other.

3. MAKING THE BEST OF IT

So now the bird set the table, and the mouse looked after the food. The mouse thought she could prepare it in the same way as the sausage, by rolling in and out among the vegetables to salt and butter them, she jumped into the pot; but she stopped short long before she reached the bottom, having already parted not only with her skin and hair, but also with her life.

Presently the bird came in and wanted to serve up dinner, but he could nowhere see the cook. In his alarm and flurry, he threw the wood here and there about the floor, called and searched, but no cook was to be found. Then some of the wood that had been carelessly thrown down caught fire and began to blaze. The bird hastened to fetch some water, but his pail fell into the well, and he fell in after it. Since he was unable to recover himself, he was drowned.

FINIS

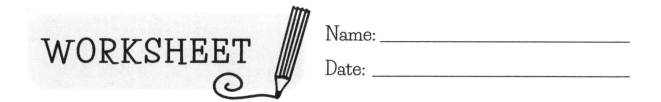

Story 10: The Mouse, the Bird, and the Sausage

I. VOCABULARY

Underline the following words in the fable and define them below.

1. partnership: _____

2. sneered: _____

3. delightful: _____

4. influenced: _____

5. seized: _____

6. hastened: _____

II. PLOT

Write simple sentences to describe the main actions in each scene.

1. Fowl Discontent

a. _____

b. _____

c. _____

d. _____

e. _____

f. _____

g. _____

2. Content Canine

a. _____

b. _____

c. _____

d. _____

e. _____

f. _____

g. _____

3. Making the Best of It

a. _____

b. _____

c. _____

d. _____

e. _____

f. _____

III. CHARACTERS

List the main characters and write a few descriptive words for each.

_____

_____

_____

_____

_____

_____

IV. IMITATION

Rewrite "The Mouse, the Bird, and the Sausage"—first and second drafts.

- Be sure to include and underline all of the vocabulary words.
- Write three separate paragraphs, one for each scene (indent three times).

Bonus Challenge: This is a pretty funny story already, but see what happens if you make the characters machines, instead of animals/food.

Story 11:
The Elves and the Cobbler

by the Brothers Grimm

1. Mysterious Help

There was once a cobbler who worked very hard and was very honest. However, he could never earn enough to live upon, and at last all he had in the world was gone except for just enough leather to make one pair of shoes.

So he cut his leather out, all ready to make up the next day, and he went to bed, meaning to rise early in the morning to finish his work. His conscience was clear and his heart light amidst all his troubles, so he went peaceably to bed, left all his cares to Heaven, and soon fell asleep. In the morning, after he had said his prayers, he sat himself down to his work, when, to his great wonder, he saw the shoes, already made, upon the table. The good man knew not what to say or think at such an odd thing happening. He looked at the workmanship: there was not one false stitch in the whole job. It was all so neat and true that the shoes were quite a masterpiece.

HISTORY

This fairy tale appears in the original 1812 *Grimms' Fairy Tales* and is a folktale from Germany. Elves used to be thought of as demons or evil spirits that would cause troubles for humans, but by the time of Grimm's fairy tales they were thought of as small people who could be good or evil. The Grimm brothers describe them as dwarfs.

The same day, a customer came in, and the shoes suited him so well that he willingly paid a price higher than usual for them, and the poor shoemaker used the money to buy enough leather to make two more pairs. In the evening, he cut out the work and went to bed early so that he could get up and begin early on the next day. However, he was saved all the trouble, for when he got up in the morning the work was already done. Soon, in came buyers, who paid him handsomely for his goods, so that he bought enough leather for four more pairs.

He cut out the work again overnight and found it done in the morning, as before, and so it went on for some time. What had been prepared in the evening was always done by daybreak, and the good man soon became prosperous and well off again.

2. The Discovery

One evening, about Christmastime, as he and his wife were sitting over the fire chatting together, he said to her, "I should like to sit up and watch tonight, that we may see who it is that comes and does my work for me." The wife liked the thought; so they left a light burning and hid themselves in a corner of the room behind a curtain that was hung up there and watched what would happen.

As soon as it was midnight there came in two little naked dwarfs; and they sat themselves upon the shoemaker's bench, took up all the work that was cut out, and began to ply with their little fingers, stitching and rapping and tapping away at such a speed that the shoemaker could not take his eyes off them. And so they went till the job was completely done and the shoes stood ready for use upon the table. This was long before daybreak; and then they bustled away as quick as lightning.

The next day the wife said to the shoemaker: "These little wights have made us rich, and we ought to be thankful to them and to do them a good turn if we can. I am quite sorry to see them run about as they do, and indeed it is not very good for them, since they have nothing upon their backs to keep off the cold. I'll tell you what: I will make each of them a shirt and a coat and waistcoat and a pair of pantaloons, and you can make each of them a little pair of shoes."

The thought pleased the good cobbler very much; and one evening, when all the things were ready, they laid them on the table, instead of the work that they used to cut out, and then went and hid themselves, to watch what the little elves would do.

3. Highly Delighted

About midnight in they came, dancing and skipping, hopped round the room, and then went to sit down to their work as usual. But when they saw the clothes lying for them, they laughed and chuckled and seemed highly delighted.

Then they dressed themselves in the twinkling of an eye and danced and capered and sprang about, as merry as could be; till at last they danced out at the door and away over the hill. The good couple saw them no more; but everything went well with them from that time forward as long as they lived.

FINIS

WORKSHEET

Name: _____

Date: _____

Story 11: The Elves and the Cobbler

I. VOCABULARY

Underline the following words in the fable and define them below.

1. cobbler: _____

2. masterpiece: _____

3. daybreak: _____

4. wights: _____

5. pantaloons: _____

6. caper: _____

II. PLOT

Write simple sentences to describe the main actions in each scene.

1. Mysterious Help

a. _____

b. _____

c. _____

d. _____

e. _____

f. _____

g. _____

2. The Discovery

a. _____

b. _____

c. _____

d. _____

e. _____

f. _____

g. _____

3. Highly Delighted

a. _____

b. _____

c. _____

d. _____

III. CHARACTERS

List the main characters and write a few descriptive words for each.

_____

_____

_____

_____

_____

_____

IV. IMITATION

Rewrite "The Elves and the Cobbler"—first and second drafts.

- Be sure to include and underline all of the vocabulary words.
- Write three separate paragraphs, one for each scene (indent three times).

Bonus Challenge: Try using a different set of magical creatures!

Story 12:
The Wolf and the Seven Little Kids

by the Brothers Grimm

1. Home Alone

There was once upon a time an old goat who had seven little kids and loved them with all the love of a mother for her children. One day she wanted to go into the forest and fetch some food. So she called all seven to her and said, "Dear children, I have to go into the forest. Be on your guard against the wolf; if he comes in, he will devour you all—skin, hair, and everything. The wretch often disguises himself, but you will know him at once by his rough voice and his black feet."

The kids said, "Dear mother, we will take good care of ourselves; you may go away without any anxiety." Then the old mother bleated and went on her way with an easy mind.

2. Wolf at the Door

It was not long before someone knocked at the house-door and called. "Open the door, dear children; your mother is here and has brought something back with her for each of you."

HISTORY

The story of "The Wolf and the Seven Little Kids" is another of Grimm's fairy tales that came from Marie Hassenpflug. She also was the source for stories such as Little Red Riding Hood, Sleeping Beauty, and Snow White. All of these types of stories have a wicked stranger (either a witch or a wolf) that causes harm to the hero..

But the little kids knew that it was the wolf by the rough voice. "We will not open the door," they cried. "You are not our mother. She has a soft, pleasant voice, but your voice is rough; you are the wolf."

Then the wolf went away to a shopkeeper and bought himself a great lump of chalk, ate this, and made his voice soft with it. He then came back, knocked at the door of the house, and called, "Open the door, dear children: your mother is here and has brought something back with her for each of you."

But the wolf had laid his black paws against the window, and the children saw them and cried, "We will not open the door, our mother has not black feet like you: you are the wolf!"

Then the wolf ran to a baker and said, "I have hurt my feet, rub some dough over them for me and sprinkle some white meal on them."

This made his paws white for him. So now the wretch went for the third time to the house-door, knocked at it, and said. "Open the door for me, children. Your dear little mother has come home and has brought every one of you something back from the forest with her."

The little kids cried, "First show us your paws that we may know if you are our dear little mother."

Then he put his paws in through the window, and when the kids saw that they were white, they believed that all he said was true and opened the door. But who should come in but the wolf! They were terrified and wanted to hide themselves. One sprang under the table, the second into the bed, the third into the stove, the fourth into the kitchen, the fifth into the cupboard, the sixth under the washing-bowl, and the seventh into the clock case. But the wolf found them all and did not hesitate; one after the other he swallowed them down his throat. The youngest, who was in the clock case, was the only one he did not find. When the wolf had satisfied his appetite he laid himself down under a tree in the green meadow outside, and began to sleep.

3. Mother Returns

Soon afterward, the old goat came home again from the forest. Ah! What a sight she saw there! The house-door stood wide open. The table, chairs, and benches were thrown down, the washing bowl lay broken to pieces, and the quilts and pillows had been pulled off the bed. She sought her children, but they were nowhere to be found. She called them one after another by name, but no one answered.

At last, when she came to the youngest, a soft voice cried, "Dear mother, I am in the clock case."

She took the kid out, and he told her that the wolf had come and had eaten all the others. Then, you may imagine how she wept over her poor children. Presently she went out of the house in her grief, and the youngest kid ran with her. When they came to the meadow, there lay the wolf by the tree, snoring so loudly that the branches shook. She looked at him on every side and saw that something was moving and struggling in his gorged belly. "Ah, heavens," she said, "is it possible that my poor children, whom he has swallowed down for his supper, can be still alive?"

Then the kid ran home and fetch scissors and a needle and thread. The goat cut open the monster's stomach, and barely had she make one cut than one little kid thrust his head out, and when she cut farther, all six sprang out one after another and were all still alive and had suffered no injury whatsoever, for in his greediness the monster had swallowed them down whole.

What rejoicing there was! They embraced their dear mother and jumped up and down. The mother, however, said, "Now go and look for some big stones, and we will fill the wicked beast's stomach with them while he is still asleep."

Then the seven kids dragged the stones there very quickly and put as many of them into his stomach as they could get in. The mother sewed him up again in great haste, so that he was not aware of anything and never once stirred.

When the wolf had enjoyed his fill of sleep, he got on his legs, and as the stones in his stomach made him very thirsty, he wanted to go to a well to drink. But when he began to walk and move about, the stones in his stomach knocked against each other and rattled. Then cried he:

"What rumbles and tumbles
Against my poor bones?
I thought 'twas six kids,
But it feels like big stones."

And when he got to the well and stooped over the water to drink, the heavy stones made him fall in, and he drowned miserably. When the seven kids saw that, they came running to the spot and cried aloud, "The wolf is dead! The wolf is dead!" and danced for joy round about the well with their mother.

FINIS

WORKSHEET

Name: _____

Date: _____

Story 12: The Wolf and the Seven Little Kids

I. VOCABULARY

Underline the following words in the fable and define them below.

1. fetch: _____

2. devour: _____

3. anxiety: _____

4. appetite: _____

5. gorged: _____

6. haste: _____

II. PLOT

Write simple sentences to describe the main actions in each scene.

1. Home Alone

a. _____

b. _____

c. _____

d. _____

2. Wolf at the Door

a. _____

b. _____

c. _____

d. _____

e. _____

f. _____

g. _____

h. _____

3. Mother Returns

a. _____

b. _____

c. _____

d. _____

e. _____

f. _____

g. _____

h. _____

III. CHARACTERS

List the main characters and write a few descriptive words for each.

_____

_____

_____

_____

_____

_____

IV. IMITATION

Rewrite "The Wolf and the Seven Little Kids"—first and second drafts.

- Be sure to include and underline all of the vocabulary words.

- Write three separate paragraphs, one for each scene (indent three times).

Bonus Challenge: Change the ways the goats can recognize the wolf.

Story 13:
The Three Children of Fortune

by the Brothers Grimm

1. The Inheritance

Once upon a time a father sent for his three sons and gave to the eldest a cock, to the second a scythe, and to the third a cat. "I am now old," said he; "my end is approaching, and I wish to provide for you before I die. Money I have none, and what I give you seems of little worth; yet it rests with you alone to use my gifts well. Only seek out for a land where nobody has the gifts that you have, and your fortune will made."

2. Rare Value

After the death of the father, the oldest set out with his cock, but wherever he went, in every town he saw from afar off, a cock sitting upon the church steeple and turning round with the wind. In the villages he always heard plenty of them crowing, and his bird was therefore nothing new; so there did not seem much chance of his making his fortune. Eventually, it happened that he came to an island where the people who lived there had never

HISTORY

This is another story about three sons, each given a special gift that helps them to survive. This is a story about inheritance and often the things that we don't value are the things that are the most important to us. What are some of the gifts that your parents have given you that you will use for the rest of your life?

heard of a cock and did not even know how to tell the time.

They knew, indeed, if it were morning or evening, but at night, if they lay awake, they had no way of knowing the time. "Behold," said he to them, "what a noble animal this is! How like a knight he is! He carries a bright red crest upon his head and spurs upon his heels! He crows three times every night at certain hours, and at the third time the sun is about to rise. But this is not all; sometimes he screams in broad daylight, and then you must take warning, for the weather is surely about to change."

This pleased the natives mightily; they kept awake for a whole night and heard, to their great joy, how gloriously the cock announced the hour, at two, four, and six o'clock. Then they asked him whether the bird was to be sold and how much he would sell it for. "About as much gold as a donkey can carry," said he.

"A very fair price for such an animal," cried they with one voice; and they agreed to give him what he asked.

When he returned home with his wealth, his brothers were amazed, and the second said, "I will now set forth too and see if I can use my scythe just as well." There did not seem, however, much of a chance of this, for no matter where he went, he was met by peasants who had as good a scythe on their shoulders as he did. But at last, as good luck would have it, he came to an island where the people had never heard of a scythe. There, as soon as the wheat was ripe, they went into the fields and pulled it up, but this was very hard work, and a great deal of it was lost. The man then set to work with his scythe and mowed down their whole crop so quickly that the people stood staring open-mouthed with wonder. They were willing to give him what he asked for such a marvelous thing, but he only took a horse laden with as much gold as it could carry.

Now the third brother had a great longing to go and see what he could do with his cat. So he set out, and at first the same thing happened to him as had happened to the others. So long as he kept upon the mainland, he met with no success. At last he passed over to an island, where, luckily for him, nobody had ever seen a cat, and they were so overrun with mice that the little wretches danced upon the tables and chairs whether the master of the house was at home or not. The people complained loudly of this nuisance. The king himself did not know how to rid himself of them in his palace; in every corner, mice were squeaking, and they gnawed everything that their teeth could lay hold of. Here was a fine field for Puss. She soon began her chase and had cleared two rooms in the twinkling of an eye. The people begged their king to buy the wonderful animal for the good of the public at any price. The king willingly gave what the third brother asked—one mule laden with gold and another with jewels. Thus the third brother returned home with a richer prize than each of the others.

3. The Cost of Ignorance

Meantime the cat feasted away upon the mice in the royal palace and devoured so many that they were no longer in any great numbers. After a while, quite spent and tired with her work, she became extremely thirsty; so she stood still, drew up her head, and cried, "Meow, Meow!"

The king gathered all his subjects when they heard this strange cry, and many ran shrieking in a great fright out of the palace. But the king held a council outside the castle about what was best to be done, and it was eventually decided to send a herald to the cat to warn her to leave the castle forthwith, or force would be used to remove her. "For," said the counselors, "we would far more willingly put up with the mice (since we are used to that evil), than to get rid of them at the risk of our lives."

A page accordingly went and asked the cat whether she was willing to leave the castle. But Puss, whose thirst became every moment more and more pressing, answered nothing but "Meow! Meow!" which the page interpreted to mean, "No! No!" and therefore carried this answer to the king. "Well," said the counselors, "then we must try what force will do." So the guns were planted, and the palace was fired upon from all sides. When the fire reached the room where the cat was she sprang out of the window and ran away; but the besiegers did not see her and went on firing until the whole palace was burned to the ground.

FINIS

Name: _____

Date: _____

Story 13: The Three Children of Fortune

I. VOCABULARY

Underline the following words in the fable and define them below.

1. cock: _____

2. scythe: _____

3. laden: _____

4. gnawed: _____

5. herald: _____

6. forthwith: _____

II. PLOT

Write simple sentences to describe the main actions in each scene.

1. The Inheritance

a. _____

b. _____

c. _____

d. _____

e. _____

2. Rare Value

a. _____

b. _____

c. _____

d. _____

e. _____

f. _____

g. _____

3. The Cost of Ignorance

a. _____

b. _____

c. _____

d. _____

e. _____

f. _____

g. _____

III. CHARACTERS

List the main characters and write a few descriptive words for each.

_____

_____

_____

_____

_____

_____

IV. IMITATION

Rewrite "The Three Children of Fortune"—first and second drafts.

- Be sure to include and underline all of the vocabulary words.

- Write three separate paragraphs, one for each scene (indent three times).

Bonus Challenge: Make your version a science fiction saga with the king as a space alien and the mice as space monsters.

Story 14:
The Frog Prince

by the Brothers Grimm

1. Promise Made

One fine evening a young princess put on her bonnet and clogs and went out to take a walk by herself in a wood. When she came to a cool spring of water that rose in the midst of the wood, she sat herself down to rest a while. Now she had a golden ball in her hand, which was her favorite plaything, and she was always tossing it up into the air and catching it again as it fell. After a time she threw it up so high that she missed catching it as it fell, and the ball bounded away and rolled along upon the ground till at last it fell down into the spring. The princess looked into the spring after her ball, but it was very deep, so deep that she could not see the bottom of it. Then she began to cry over her loss and said, "Alas, if I could only get my ball again I would give all my fine clothes and jewels, and everything that I had in the world."

Whilst she was speaking a frog put its head out of the water and said, "Princess, why do you weep so bitterly?"

HISTORY

This is the first story in the Brothers Grimm collection: they loved this story a lot. Notice how similar it is to the story of "Beauty and the Beast." It is also a story about keeping your word despite how difficult it may be.

"Alas!" said she, "what can you do for me you nasty frog? My golden ball has fallen into the spring."

The frog said, "I do not want your pearls and jewels and fine clothes, but if you will befriend me and let me live with you and eat from off your golden plate and sleep upon your pillow, I will bring you your ball again."

"What nonsense," thought the princess, "this silly frog is talking! He can never even get out of the spring to visit me, though he may be able to get my ball for me, and therefore I will tell him he shall have what he asks." So she said to the frog, "Well, if you will bring me my ball, I will do all you ask."

Then the frog put his head down and dived deep under the water. After a little while he came up again with the ball in his mouth and threw it on the edge of the spring. As soon as the young princess saw her ball, she ran to pick it up. She was so overjoyed to have it in her hand again that she never thought of the frog but ran home with it as fast as she could. The frog called after her, "Stay, princess, and take me with you as you said." But she did not stop to hear a word.

2. Promise Kept

The next day, when the King's daughter was sitting at table with the King and all the court and eating from her golden plate, there came something pitter-pattering up the marble stairs, and then there came a knocking at the door and a voice crying, "Youngest King's daughter, let me in!"

And she got up and ran to see who it could be, but when she opened the door, there was the frog sitting outside. Then she shut the door hastily and went back to her seat, feeling very uneasy. The King noticed how pale her face had turned and said, "My child, what are you afraid of? Is there a giant standing at the door ready to carry you away?"

"Oh no," answered she; "no giant, but a horrid frog."

"And what does the frog want?" asked the King.

"O dear father," answered she, "when I was sitting by the well yesterday and playing with my golden ball, it fell into the water, and while I was crying for the loss of it, the frog came and got it again for me on condition that I would let him be my companion, but I never thought that he could leave the water and come after me. But now there he is outside the door, and he wants to come in."

And then they all heard him knocking the second time and crying,

"Young King's daughter,
Open to me!
By the well water
What promised you me?
Young King's daughter
Now open to me!"

Then the king said to the young princess, "That which thou hast promised thou must perform, so go and let him in."

She did so, and the frog hopped in, following at her heels, till she reached her chair. Then he stopped and cried, "Pray lift me upon a chair, and let me sit next to you." As soon as she had done this, the frog said, "Put your plate nearer to me, so that I may eat out of it." This she did, and when he had eaten as much as he could, he said, "Now I am tired; carry me upstairs, and put me on your pillow."

Then the King's daughter began to weep and was afraid of the cold frog, because nothing would satisfy him but he must sleep in her pretty clean bed.

Now the King grew angry with her saying, "That which thou hast promised in thy time of necessity, must thou now perform."

And the princess, though very unwilling, took him up with her finger and thumb, carried him upstairs, and put him on her pillow, where he slept all night long. As soon as it was light he jumped up, hopped downstairs and went out of the house. "Now, then," thought the princess, "at last he is gone, and I shall be troubled with him no more."

But she was mistaken, for when night came again she heard the same tapping at the door, and the frog came once more and said,

"Young King's daughter,
Open to me!
By the well water
What promised you me?
Young King's daughter
Now open to me!"

3. Charm Broken

When the princess opened the door, the frog came in and slept upon her pillow as before, till the morning broke. And the third night he did the same. But when the princess awoke on the following morning she was astonished to see, instead of the frog, a handsome prince, gazing out the window with the most beautiful eyes she had ever seen.

He told her that he had been enchanted by a spiteful fairy, who had changed him into a frog; and that he had been fated to remain a frog till some princess should take him out of the spring and befriend him for three nights. "You," said the prince, "have broken this cruel charm, and now I have nothing to wish for but that you should go with me into my father's kingdom, where I will marry you and love you as long as you live."

And it came to pass that, with her father's consent, they became bride and bridegroom and lived happily a great many years.

FINIS

Name: _____

Date: _____

Story 14: The Frog Prince

I. VOCABULARY

Underline the following words in the fable and define them below.

1. bonnet: _____

2. clogs: _____

3. hastily: _____

4. horrid: _____

5. necessity: _____

6. spiteful: _____

II. PLOT

Write simple sentences to describe the main actions in each scene.

1. Promise Made

a. _____

b. _____

c. _____

d. _____

e. _____

2. Promise Kept

a. _____

b. _____

c. _____

d. _____

e. _____

3. Charm Broken

a. _____

b. _____

c. _____

d. _____

e. _____

III. CHARACTERS

List the main characters and write a few descriptive words for each.

_____

_____

_____

_____

_____

_____

IV. IMITATION

Rewrite "The Frog Prince"—first and second drafts.

- Be sure to include and underline all of the vocabulary words.
- Write three separate paragraphs, one for each scene (indent three times).

Bonus Challenge: Use a different animal and a different set of tasks.

Story 15:
The Golden Goose

by the Brothers Grimm

1. Three Sons

There once was a man who had three sons. The youngest was called Dummling—which is much the same as Dunderhead, for all thought he was more than half a fool—and he was at all times mocked and badly treated by the whole household.

It happened that the eldest son took it into his head one day to go into the forest to cut firewood. His mother gave him a nice meat pie and a bottle of wine to take with him that he might refresh himself at his work. As he went into the wood, a little old man wished him a good day and said, "Give me a little piece of meat from your plate and a little wine out of your flask, for I am very hungry and thirsty."

But this clever young man said: "Give you my meat and wine? No, I thank you, I should not have enough left for myself," and away he went.

He soon began to cut down a tree; but he had not worked long before he missed his stroke and cut himself and was forced to go home to

HISTORY

This is another story about three brothers, and the third brother saves the day! In this story, the golden goose is often considered to be an image of the dangers of greed.

have the wound dressed. Now it was the little old man that sent him this mischief.

The next day, the second son went out to work, and his mother gave him, too, a meat pie and a bottle of wine. And the same little old man met him also and asked him for something to eat and drink. But he, too, thought himself very clever and said, "The more you eat, the less there would be for me, so go your way!"

The little man took care that he, too, should have his reward, and the second stroke that he aimed against a tree hit him on the leg, so that he, too, was forced to go home.

Then Dummling said, "Father, I should like to go and cut wood, too." But his father said, "Your brothers have both lamed themselves. You had better stay at home, for you know nothing about the business of woodcutting."

But Dummling was very pressing, and at last his father said, "Go your way! You will be wiser when you have gotten the reward of your folly."

And his mother gave him only some dry bread and a bottle of sour beer. But when he went into the wood he met the little old man, who said, "Give me some meat and drink, for I am very hungry and thirsty."

Dummling said, "I have only dry bread and sour beer; if that will suit you, we will sit down and eat it, such as it is, together."

So they sat down; and when the lad pulled out his bread, behold, it had turned into a rich meat pie, and his sour beer, when they tasted it, was delightful wine. They ate and drank heartily, and when they were finished, the little man said, "Since you have a kind heart and have been willing to share everything with me, I will send a blessing upon you. There stands an old tree: cut it down, and you will find something at the root."

Then he took his leave and went his way.

2. Golden Goose

Dummling set to work and cut down the tree. When it fell, he found, in a hollow under the roots, a goose with feathers of pure gold. He took it up and went on to a little inn by the roadside, where he intended to sleep for the night on his way home.

Now the landlord had three daughters; and when they saw the goose they were very eager to learn what this wonderful bird could be and wished very much to pluck one of the feathers out of its tail.

At last the eldest said, "I must and will have a feather."

So she waited till Dummling had gone to bed and then seized the goose by the wing, but to her great wonder there she stuck, for she could get neither hand nor finger away again. Then in came the second sister and she wanted a feather, too, but the moment she touched her sister, there she too hung fast. At last came the third, and she also wanted a feather, but the other two cried out: "Keep away! For Heaven's sake, keep away!"

However, she did not understand what they meant. "If they are there," thought she, "I may as well be there too." So she went up to them; but the moment she touched her sisters she stuck fast and hung to the goose as they did. And so they kept company with the goose all night in the cold.

The next morning Dummling got up and carried off the goose under his arm. He took no notice at all of the three girls but went out with them sticking fast behind. So where he traveled, they too were forced to follow, whether they wished to or not, as fast as their legs could carry them.

In the middle of a field the parson met them; and when he saw the train he said: "Are you not ashamed of yourselves, you bold girls, to run after a young man in that way over the fields? Is that good behavior?"

Then he took the youngest by the hand to lead her away; but as soon as he touched her he too hung fast and followed in the company; though much against his will, for he was not only not in a good condition for running fast, but just then he had a little touch of the gout in the great toe of his right foot.

By and by up came the clerk, and when he saw his master, the parson, running after the three girls, he was greatly astonished and said, "Holla! Holla! your reverence! where so fast? There is a christening today." Then he ran up and took him by the gown; when, lo and behold! he stuck fast too.

As the five were thus trudging along, one behind another, they met two laborers with their mattocks coming from work; and the parson cried out loudly to them to help him. But scarcely had they laid hands on him when they too fell into the row; and so they made seven, all running together after Dummling and his goose.

3. Traveling Train

Now Dummling thought he would see a little of the world before he went home, so he and his train journeyed on, till at last they came to a city where there was a king who had only one child—a daughter. The princess was so thoughtful and moody that no one could make her laugh, and the king had made known to all the world that whoever could make her laugh should have her for his wife.

When the young man heard this, he went to her, with his goose and its whole troupe behind it, and soon as she saw the seven all hanging together and running along, treading on one another's heels, she could not help bursting into a long and loud laugh. Then Dummling claimed her for his wife and married her, and he was heir to the kingdom and lived long and happily with his wife.

But what became of the goose and the goose's wing I never could hear.

FINIS

WORKSHEET

Name: _____

Date: _____

Story 15: The Golden Goose

I. VOCABULARY

Underline the following words in the fable and define them below.

1. mocked: _____

2. mischief: _____

3. seized: _____

4. fast: _____

5. trudging: _____

6. mattocks: _____

II. PLOT

Write simple sentences to describe the main actions in each scene.

1. Three Sons

a. _____

b. _____

c. _____

d. _____

e. _____

f. _____

g. _____

2. Golden Goose

a. _____

b. _____

c. _____

d. _____

e. _____

f. _____

g. _____

3. Traveling Train

a. _____

b. _____

c. _____

d. _____

e. _____

f. _____

III. CHARACTERS

List the main characters and write a few descriptive words for each.

_____

_____

_____

_____

_____

_____

IV. IMITATION

Rewrite "The Golden Goose"—first and second drafts.

- Be sure to include and underline all of the vocabulary words.

- Write three separate paragraphs, one for each scene (indent three times).

Bonus Challenge: Use a different animal than a golden goose, but make sure that it is clearly a symbol of something else. For example, you could use a giant lion to symbolize power or a chocolate pig to symbolize gluttony.

Story 16:
The Man in the Bag

by the Brothers Grimm

1. Prince of Turnips

There were two brothers who were both soldiers; the one had grown rich, but the other had no luck and was very poor. The poor man thought he would try to better himself; so pulling off his red coat, he became a gardener and dug his ground well and sowed turnips.

When the crop came up there was one plant bigger than all the rest, and it kept getting larger and larger and seemed as if it would never stop growing, so that it might have been called the prince of turnips, for there never was such a one seen before and never will be again. At last it was so big that it filled a cart, and two oxen could hardly draw it, but the gardener did not know what in the world to do with it, nor whether it would be a blessing or a curse to him. One day he said to himself: "What shall I do with it? If I sell it, it will bring no more than another would; and as for eating, the little turnips I am sure are better than this great one;

HISTORY

This is a trickster story, much like "The Tar-Baby" in the Uncle Remus story or "Puss in Boots" or *Tom Sawyer*.

the best thing perhaps that I can do will be to give it to the king as a mark of my respect."

Then he yoked his oxen and drew the turnip to the court and gave it to the king. "What a wonderful thing!" said the king. "I have seen many strange things in my life, but such a monster as this I never saw before. Where did you get the seed, or is it only your good luck? If so, you are a true child of fortune."

"Ah, no!" answered the gardener, "I am no child of fortune; I am a poor soldier who never yet could get enough to live upon, so I set to work tilling the ground. I have a brother who is rich, and your majesty knows him well, and all the world knows him, but because I am poor, everybody forgets me."

Then the king took pity on him and said: "You shall be poor no longer. I will give you so much that you shall be even richer than your brother." So he gave him money and lands and flocks and herds and made him so rich that his brother's wealth could not at all be compared with his.

2. A Brother's Envy

When the brother heard of all this and how a turnip had made the gardener so rich, he envied him much and considered how he could please the king and get the same good luck for himself.

However, he thought he would manage more cleverly than his brother, so he got together a rich gift of jewels and fine horses for the king, thinking that he would receive a much larger gift in return; for if his brother had so much given him for a turnip, what must his gift be worth?

The king took the gift very graciously and said he knew not what he could give in return more costly and wonderful than the great turnip. The soldier was forced to put it into a cart and drag it home with him. When he reached home, he knew not upon whom to vent his rage and envy. At length wicked thoughts came into his head, and he sought to kill his brother.

So he hired some villains to murder him. Having shown them where to lie in ambush, he went to his brother and said: "O dear brother, I have found a hidden treasure; let us go and dig it up and share it between us." The other had no thought or fear of his brother's roguery, so they went out together.

As they were traveling along the murderers rushed out upon him, bound him, and were going to hang him on a tree.

But while they were getting everything ready, they heard the trampling of a horse afar off, which so frightened them that they pushed their prisoner neck and shoulders together into a sack and swung him up by a cord to the tree, where they left him dangling and ran away, meaning to come back and kill him in the evening.

3. Sack of Wisdom

Meantime, however, the gardener worked and worked away, till he had made a hole large enough to put out his head. When the horseman came up, he turned out to be a student, a merry fellow, who was journeying along on his nag and singing as he went. As soon as the man in the bag saw him passing under the tree, he cried out: "Good morning! Good morning to you, my friend!" The student looked about and, seeing no one, and not knowing where the voice came from, cried out, "Who calls me?"

Then the man in the bag cried out: "Lift up your eyes, for behold here I sit in the sack of wisdom! Here have I, in a short time, learned great and wondrous things. Compared to what is taught in this seat, all the learning of the schools is empty air. A little longer and I shall know all that man can know and shall come out wiser than the wisest of mankind. Here I discern the signs and motions of the heavens and the stars; the laws that control the winds; the number of the sands on the seashore; the healing of the sick; the virtues of all medicines, of birds, and of precious stones. If only you were here just once, my friend, you would soon feel the power of knowledge."

The student listened to all this and wondered much. At last he said: "Blessed be the day and hour when I found you. Can't you let me into the sack for a little while?" Then the other answered, as if very unwilling: "For a short time, I may allow you to sit here, if you will reward me well and treat me kindly, but you must wait for an hour below, till I have learned some little things that are yet unknown to me."

So the student sat himself down and waited awhile, but he grew impatient, and he begged hard that he might ascend immediately, for his thirst of knowledge was very great. Then the other began to give way and said: "You must let the bag of wisdom descend, by untying yonder cord, and then you shall enter." So the student let him down, opened the bag, and set him free. "Now then," cried he, "let me mount quickly!" As he began to put himself into the sack heels first, "Wait a while!" said the gardener; "that is not the way." Then he pushed him in head first, tied up the bag's mouth, and soon swung up the searcher after wisdom, dangling in the air. "How is it with you, friend?" said he. "Do you not feel that wisdom comes unto you? Rest there in peace till you are a wiser man than you were."

So saying, he borrowed the student's nag to ride home upon and trotted off as fast as he could for fear the villains should return; and he left the poor student to gather wisdom, till somebody should come and let him down, when he had found out in which posture he was wisest—on his head or his heels.

FINIS

WORKSHEET

Name: _____

Date: _____

Story 16: The Man in the Bag

I. VOCABULARY

Underline the following words in the fable and define them below.

1. sow: _____

2. yoked: _____

3. villains: _____

4. roguery: _____

5. ascend: _____

6. nag: _____

II. PLOT

Write simple sentences to describe the main actions in each scene.

1. Prince of Turnips

a. _____

b. _____

c. _____

d. _____

e. _____

2. A Brother's Envy

a. _____

b. _____

c. _____

d. _____

e. _____

f. _____

3. Sack of Wisdom

a. _____

b. _____

c. _____

d. _____

e. _____

f. _____

III. CHARACTERS

List the main characters and write a few descriptive words for each.

_____

_____

_____

_____

_____

_____

IV. IMITATION

Rewrite "The Man in the Bag"—first and second drafts.

• Be sure to include and underline all of the vocabulary words.

• Write three separate paragraphs, one for each scene (indent three times).

Bonus Challenge: Set your version in the Wild West or with animals instead of people.

Story 17: The Emperor's New Clothes

by Hans Christian Anderson

1. Excessively Fond

Many years ago there lived an Emperor who was so fond of grand new clothes that he spent all his money upon them that he might be very splendid. He did not care about his soldiers, nor about the theater, and only liked to drive out and show his new clothes. He had a coat for every hour of the day; and just as they say of a king, "He is in council," so they always said of him, "The Emperor is in the wardrobe."

In the great city in which he lived, it was always very merry; every day many strangers arrived. One day two rogues came; they said they were weavers and declared they could weave the finest stuff anyone could imagine. Not only were their colors and patterns, they said, uncommonly beautiful, but the clothes made of the stuff possessed the wonderful quality that they became invisible to anyone who was unfit for the office he held or was hopelessly stupid.

HISTORY

This is another story by Hans Christian Anderson. It is based on a 1335 Spanish collection of stories. Anderson added the ending in which the child recognizes that the emperor is not wearing anything.

"Those would be capital clothes!" thought the Emperor. "If I wore those, I should be able to find out what men in my empire are not fit for the places they have; I could tell the clever from the dunces. Yes, the stuff must be woven for me directly!"

And he gave the two rogues a great deal of cash so that they might begin their work at once. As for them, they put up two looms and pretended to be working, but they had nothing at all on their looms. They at once demanded the finest silk and the costliest gold; this they put into their own pockets and worked at the empty looms till late into the night.

2. Loom Lunacy

"I should like to know how far they have got on with the stuff," thought the Emperor. But he felt quite uncomfortable when he thought that those who were not fit for their offices could not see it.

He believed, indeed, that he had nothing to fear for himself, but he preferred first to send someone else to see how matters stood. All the people in the city knew what peculiar power the stuff possessed, and all were anxious to see how bad or how stupid their neighbors were.

"I will send my honest old Minister to the weavers," thought the Emperor. "He can judge best how the stuff looks, for he has sense, and no one understands his office better than he."

Now the good old Minister went out into the hall where the two rogues sat working at the empty looms. "Mercy on us!" thought the old Minister, and he opened his eyes wide. "I cannot see anything at all!" But he did not say this.

Both the rogues begged him to be so good as to come nearer and asked if he did not approve of the colors and the pattern. Then they pointed to the empty loom, and the poor old Minister went on opening and closing his eyes; but he could see nothing, for there was nothing to see.

"Mercy!" thought he, "can I indeed be so stupid? I never thought that, and not a soul must know it. Am I not fit for my office? No, it will never do for me to tell that I could not see the stuff."

"Don't you say anything to it?" asked one, as he went on weaving.

"Oh, it is charming—quite enchanting!" answered the old Minister, as he peered through his spectacles. "What a fine pattern, and what colors! Yes, I shall tell the Emperor that I am very much pleased with it."

"Well, we are glad of that," said both the weavers; and then they named the colors and explained the strange pattern. The old Minister listened attentively, that he might be able to repeat it when the Emperor came. And he did so.

Now the rogues asked for more money, and silk and gold which they said they wanted for weaving. They put it all into their own pockets, and not a thread was put upon the loom; they continued to work at the empty frames as before.

All the people in the town were talking about the gorgeous stuff. The Emperor wished to see it himself while it was still upon the loom. With a whole crowd of chosen men, among whom was also the honest statesman who had already been there, he went to the two cunning rogues who were now weaving without fiber or thread.

"Is not that splendid?" said the statesman, who had already been there once.

"What's this?" thought the Emperor. "I can see nothing at all! That is terrible. Am I stupid? Am I not fit to be Emperor? That would be the most dreadful thing that could happen to me." So he said aloud, "Oh, it is very pretty! It has our highest approval." And he nodded in a contented way and gazed at the empty loom, for he would not say that he saw nothing. The whole suite whom he had with him looked and looked and saw nothing anymore than the rest, but, like the Emperor, they said, "That is pretty!" and counseled him to wear the splendid new clothes for the first time at the great procession that was about to take place. "It is splendid, excellent!" went from mouth to mouth. On all sides there seemed to be general rejoicing, and the Emperor gave the rogues the title of Imperial Court Weavers.

3. Words of the Innocent

The whole night before the morning on which the procession was to take place the rogues were up and kept more than sixteen candles burning. The people could see that they were hard at work completing the Emperor's new clothes. They pretended to take the stuff down from the looms; they made cuts in the air with great scissors; they sewed with needles without thread; and at last they said, "Now the clothes are ready!"

The Emperor came himself with his noblest cavaliers; and the two rogues lifted up one arm as if they were holding something and said: "See, here are the trousers! Here is the coat! Here is the cloak!" and so on. "It is as light as a spider's web. One would think one had nothing on, but that is just the beauty of it."

"Yes," said all the cavaliers; but they could not see anything, for nothing was there.

"Will your Imperial Majesty please to conde-scend to take off your clothes?" said the rogues. "Then we will put on the new clothes here in front of the great mirror."

The Emperor took off his clothes, and the rogues pretended to put on him each new gar-ment as it was ready; and the Emperor turned round and round before the mirror.

"Oh, how well they look! How capitally they fit!" said all.

"What a pattern! What colors! That is a splen-did dress!"

"They are standing outside with the cano-py which is to be borne above your Majesty in the procession!" announced the Head Master of the ceremonies.

"Well, I am ready," replied the Emperor. "Does it not suit me well?" And then he turned again to the mirror, for he wanted it to appear as if he contemplated his adornment with great interest.

The two chamberlains who were to carry the train stooped down with their hands toward the floor, just as if they were picking up the mantle; then they pretended to be holding something in the air.

They did not dare to let it be noticed that they saw nothing.

So the Emperor went in procession under the rich canopy, and everyone in the streets said: "How incomparable are the Emperor's new clothes! How it fits him!" No one would let it be perceived that he could see nothing, for that would have shown that he was not fit for his office or was very stupid. No clothes of the Emperor's had ever been such a success as these.

"But he has nothing on!" a little child cried out at last.

"Just hear what that innocent says!" said the father; and one whispered to another what the child had said.

"But he has nothing on!" said the whole people at length. That touched the Emperor, for it seemed to him that they were right; but he thought within himself, "I must go through with the procession." And so he held himself a little higher, and the chamberlains held on tighter than ever and carried the tail end of his robe which did not exist at all.

FINIS

Story 17: The Emperor's New Clothes

I. VOCABULARY

Underline the following words in the fable and define them below.

1. wardrobe: _____

2. rogues: _____

3. gorgeous: _____

4. procession: _____

5. canopy: _____

6. mantle: _____

II. PLOT

Write simple sentences to describe the main actions in each scene.

1. Excessively Fond

a. _____

b. _____

c. _____

d. _____

e. _____

f. _____

g. _____

2. Loom Lunacy

a. _____

b. _____

c. _____

d. _____

e. _____

f. _____

g. _____

3. Words of the Innocent

a. _____

b. _____

c. _____

d. _____

e. _____

f. _____

g. _____

III. CHARACTERS

List the main characters and write a few descriptive words for each.

_____

_____

_____

_____

_____

_____

IV. IMITATION

Rewrite "The Emperor's New Clothes"—first and second drafts.

- Be sure to include and underline all of the vocabulary words.

- Write three separate paragraphs, one for each scene (indent three times).

Bonus Challenge: Set your story in the modern world, but make sure it's something other than clothes that everybody gets fooled with.

Story 18:
King Grizzle-Beard

by the Brothers Grimm

1. Ill-Treatment

A great king of a land far away in the East had a daughter who was very beautiful but so proud and haughty and conceited that none of the princes who came to ask her hand in marriage were good enough for her, and she only made sport of them.

Once upon a time the king held a great feast and invited all her suitors. They all sat in a row ranged according to their rank—kings and princes and dukes and earls and counts and barons and knights. Then the princess came in, and as she passed by them she had something spiteful to say to everyone. The first was too fat. "He's as round as a tub," said she. The next was too tall. "What a pole!" said she. The next was too short. "What a dumpling!" said she. The fourth was too pale, and she called him "Wall-face." The fifth was too red, so she called him "Jester." And thus she had some joke to crack upon everyone; but she laughed more than all

HISTORY

This is a fairy tale which is very similar to Shakespeare's *The Taming of the Shrew* or any number of stories in which a spoiled brat is humbled and taught how to work hard.

at a good king who was there. "Look at him," said she; "his beard is like an old mop; he shall be called Grizzle-beard." So the king got the nickname of Grizzle-beard.

But the old king was very angry when he saw how his daughter behaved and how she treated all his guests, and he vowed that, willing or unwilling, she should marry the first man, be he prince or beggar, that came to the door.

2. Hard Lessons

Two days later, there came by a traveling fiddler who began to play under the window and beg alms. When the king heard him, he said, "Let him come in." So they brought in the dirty-looking fellow; and when he had sung before the king and the princess, he begged a boon. Then the king said, "You have sung so well that I will give you my daughter for your wife." The princess begged and prayed, but the king said, "I have sworn to give you to the firstcomer, and I will keep my word." So words and tears were of no avail: the parson was sent for, and the princess was married to the fiddler. When this was over the king said, "Now get ready to go—you must not stay here—you must travel on with your husband."

Then the fiddler went his way and took her with him, and they soon came to a great wood.

"Pray," said she, "whose fine wood is this?"

"It belongs to King Grizzle-beard," he answered. "Had you taken him, it would all be yours."

"Ah! I was a foolish young thing, I'm afraid!" sighed she. "I wish that I had married King Grizzle-beard!"

Next they came to some fine meadows. "Whose fine green meadows are these?" said she.

"They belong to King Grizzle-beard; had you taken him, they would all have been yours."

"Ah! I was a foolish young thing, I'm afraid!" said she. "I wish that I had married King Grizzle-beard!"

Then they came to a great city. "Whose is this noble city so fine?" said she.

"It belongs to King Grizzle-beard; had you taken him, it would all have been yours."

"Ah! I was a foolish young thing, I'm afraid!" sighed she. "Why did I not marry King Grizzle-beard?"

"That is no business of mine," said the fiddler. "Why should you wish for another husband; am not I good enough for you?"

At last they came to a small cottage. "What a paltry place!" said she. "To whom does that little dirty hole belong?"

Then the fiddler said, "That is your and my house, where we are to live."

"Where are your servants?" cried she.

"What do we want with servants?" said he. "You must do for yourself whatever is to be done. Now make the fire and put on water and cook my supper, for I am very tired."

But the princess knew nothing about making fires and cooking, and the fiddler was forced to help her. When they had eaten a very scanty meal, they went to bed, but the fiddler called her up very early in the morning to clean the house.

Thus they lived for two days. When they had eaten up all there was in the cottage, the man said, "Wife, we can't go on thus, spending money and earning nothing. You must learn to weave baskets."

Then he went out and cut willows and brought them home, and she began to weave, but it made her fingers very sore. "I see this work won't do," said he. "Try and spin; perhaps you will do that better." She sat down and tried to spin, but the threads cut her tender fingers till the blood ran. "See now," said the fiddler, "you are good for nothing; you can do no work. What a bargain I have got!

However, I'll try and set up a trade in earthenware, and you shall stand in the market and sell them."

"Alas!" sighed she, "if any of my father's court should pass by and see me standing in the market, how they will laugh at me!"

But her husband did not care for that and said she must work, if she did not wish to die of hunger. She sat herself down with the earthenware in the corner of the market; but a drunken soldier soon came by and rode his horse against her stall and broke all her goods into a thousand pieces. Then she began to cry and knew not what to do. "Ah! What will become of me?" said she. "What will my husband say?"

So she ran home and told him all. "Who would have thought you would have been so silly," said he, "as to put an earthenware stall in the corner of the market where everybody passes? But let us have no more crying; I see you are not fit for this sort of work, so I have been to the king's palace and asked if they wanted a kitchen maid. They say they will take you, and there you will have plenty to eat."

Thus the princess became a kitchen maid and helped the cook to do all the dirtiest work, but she was allowed to carry home some of the meat that was left, and on this they lived.

3. Marriage Feast

She had not been there long, before she heard that the king was passing by, going to be married.

She went to one of the windows and looked out. Everything was ready, and all the pomp and brightness of the court was there. Then she bitterly grieved for the pride and folly which had brought her so low.

And the servants gave her some of the rich meats, which she put into her basket to take home. All of a sudden, as she was going out, in came the king in golden clothes, and when he saw the beautiful woman at the door, he took her by the hand and said she should be his partner in the dance. But she trembled for fear, for she saw that it was King Grizzle-beard who was making sport of her.

However, he kept fast hold and led her in. The cover of the basket came off so that the meats in it fell all about. Then everybody laughed and jeered at her; and she was so abashed that she wished herself a thousand feet deep in the earth. She sprang to the door to run away; but on the steps King Grizzle-beard overtook her and brought her back and said: "Fear me not! I am the fiddler who has lived with you in the hut. I brought you there because I really loved you. I am also the soldier that overset your stall. I have done all this only to cure you of your silly pride and to show you the folly of your mistreatment of me. Now all is over; you have learned wisdom, and it is time to hold our marriage feast."

Then the chamberlains came and brought her the most beautiful robes. Her father and his whole court were there already and welcomed her home on her marriage. Joy was in every face and every heart. The feast was grand. They danced and sang, and all were merry. I only wish that you and I had been at that party.

FINIS

Name: _____

Date: _____

Story 18: King Grizzle-Beard

I. VOCABULARY

Underline the following words in the fable and define them below.

1. suitors: _____

2. spiteful: _____

3. boon: _____

4. paltry: _____

5. bargain: _____

6. abashed: _____

II. PLOT

Write simple sentences to describe the main actions in each scene.

1. Ill-Treatment

a. _____

b. _____

c. _____

d. _____

2. Hard Lessons

a. _____

b. _____

c. _____

d. _____

e. _____

f. _____

g. _____

3. Marriage Feast

a. _____

b. _____

c. _____

d. _____

e. _____

f. _____

g. _____

III. CHARACTERS

List the main characters and write a few descriptive words for each.

_____

_____

_____

_____

_____

_____

_____

IV. IMITATION

Rewrite "King Grizzle-Beard"—first and second drafts.

- Be sure to include and underline all of the vocabulary words.

- Write three separate paragraphs, one for each scene (indent three times).

Bonus Challenge: Change the tasks for the princess to do.

Story 19:
The Fisherman and His Wife

by the Brothers Grimm

1. Some Catch

There was once a fisherman who lived with his wife in a pigsty, close by the seaside. The fisherman used to go out fishing all day long. One day, as he sat on the shore with his rod, looking at the sparkling waves and watching his line, all of a sudden his float was dragged away deep into the water, and when he drew it up, he pulled out a great fish. But the fish said, "Pray let me live! I am not a real fish; I am an enchanted prince; put me in the water again, and let me go!" "Oh! Ho!" said the man, "you need not make so many words about the matter. I will have nothing to do with a fish that can talk, so swim away, sir, as soon as you please!" Then he put him back into the water, and the fish darted straight down to the bottom and left a long streak of blood behind him on the wave.

When the fisherman went home to his wife in the pigsty, he told her how he had caught a great fish and how it had told him it was an

HISTORY

The Brothers Grimm got this story from a painter called Philip Runge. It is another example of a story about being discontent with what you have and the problems of pride. How many of us wish that the universe would simply bow to our whims?

enchanted prince and how, on hearing it speak, he had let it go again.

"Did not you ask it for anything?" said the wife. "No," said the man. "What should I ask for?" "Ah!" said the wife, "we live very wretchedly here, in this nasty, dirty pigsty. Do go back and tell the fish we want a snug little cottage."

2. Many Boons

The fisherman did not much like the business; however, he went to the seashore, and when he arrived the water looked all yellow and green. He stood at the water's edge and said,

"O man of the sea!
Hearken to me!
My wife Ilsabill
Will have her own will,
And hath sent me to beg a boon of thee!"

Then the fish came swimming to him and said: "Well, what is her will? What does your wife want?" "Ah!" said the fisherman, "she says that when I had caught you, I ought to have asked you for something before I let you go; she does not like living any longer in the pigsty and wants a snug little cottage." "Go home, then," said the fish. "She is in the cottage already!" So the man went home and saw his wife standing at the door of a nice trim little cottage. "Come in, come in!" said she. "Is not this much better than the filthy pigsty we had?" There was a parlor and a bed chamber and a kitchen; and behind the cottage there was a little garden, planted with all sorts of flowers and fruits; and there was a courtyard behind, full of ducks and chickens. "Ah!" said the fisherman, "how happily we shall live now!" "We will try to do so, at least," said his wife.

Everything went right for a week or two, and then Dame Ilsabill said: "Husband, there is not near room enough for us in this cottage; the courtyard and the garden are a great deal too small; I should like to have a large stone castle to live in; go to the fish again and tell him to give us a castle." "Wife, he will be angry; we ought to be content with this pretty cottage to live in." "Nonsense!" said the wife; "he will do it very willingly, I know; go along and try!"

The fisherman went, but his heart was very heavy, and when he came to the sea it looked blue and gloomy, though it was very calm. He went close to the edge of the waves and said,

"O man of the sea!
Hearken to me!
My wife Ilsabill

Will have her own will,
And hath sent me to beg a boon of thee!"

"Well, what does she want now?" said the fish. "Ah!" said the man, dolefully, "my wife wants to live in a stone castle." "Go home, then," said the fish. "She is standing at the gate of it already." So away went the fisherman and found his wife standing before the gate of a great castle. "See," said she, "is not this grand?" With that they went into the castle together and found a great many servants there, and the rooms all richly furnished, and full of golden chairs and tables. Behind the castle was a garden, and around it was a park half a mile long, full of sheep and goats and hares and deer, and in the courtyard were stables and barns. "Well," said the man, now we will live cheerful and happy in this beautiful castle for the rest of our lives." "Perhaps we may," said the wife; "but let us sleep upon it before we make up our minds to that." So they went to bed.

The next morning when Dame Ilsabill awoke it was broad daylight, and she nudged the fisherman with her elbow and said, "Get up, husband, for we must be king of all the land."

"Wife, wife," said the man, "why should we wish to be king? I will not be king." "Then I will," said she.

"But wife," said the fisherman, "how can you be king? The fish cannot make you a king." "Husband," said she, "say no more about it, but go and try! I will be king." So the man went away quite sorrowful to think that his wife should want to be king. This time the sea looked a dark gray color and was covered with curling waves and ridges of foam as he cried out,

"O man of the sea!
Hearken to me!
My wife Ilsabill
Will have her own will,
And hath sent me to beg a boon of thee!"

"Well, what would she have now" said the fish. "Alas!" said the poor man, "my wife wants to be king."

"Go home," said the fish; "she is king already."

Then the fisherman went home; and as he came close to the palace he saw a troop of soldiers and heard the sound of drums and trumpets. And when he went in he saw his wife sitting on a high throne of gold and diamonds, with a golden crown upon her head; and on each side of her stood six fair maidens, each a head taller than the other. "Well, wife," said the fisherman, "are you king?" "Yes," said she, "I am king." And when he had looked at her for a long time, he said, "Ah wife! What a fine thing it is to be king! Now we shall never have anything more to wish for as long as we live." "I will think about that," said the wife. Then they went to bed; but Dame Ilsabill could not sleep all night for thinking what she should be next. At last, as she was dropping asleep, morning broke, and the sun rose. "Ha!" thought she, as she woke up and looked at it through the window, "after all I cannot prevent the sun rising." At this thought she was very angry and woke her husband, and said, "Husband, go to the fish and tell him I must be lord of the sun and moon." The fisherman was half asleep but the thought frightened him so much that he started and fell out of bed. "Alas, wife!" said he, "Can you not be content with being king?" "No," said she, "I am very uneasy as long as the sun and moon rise without my leave. Go to the fish at once!"

3. The Last Straw

Then the man went shivering with fear; and as he was going down to the shore a dreadful storm arose, so that the trees and the very rocks shook. All the heavens became black with stormy clouds and the lightnings played and the thunders rolled and you might have seen in the sea great black waves, swelling up like the mountains with crowns of white foam upon their heads. And the fisherman crept toward the sea and cried out as well as he could,

"O man of the sea!
Hearken to me!
My wife Ilsabill
Will have her own will,
And hath sent me to beg a boon of thee!"

"What does she want now?" said the fish. "Ah!" said he, "she wants to be lord of the sun and moon." "Go home," said the fish, "to your pigsty again."

And there they live to this very day.

FINIS

Name: _____

Date: _____

Story 19: The Fisherman and His Wife

I. VOCABULARY

Underline the following words in the fable and define them below.

1. pray: _____

2. enchanted: _____

3. wretchedly: _____

4. boon: _____

5. Dame: _____

6. dolefully: _____

II. PLOT

Write simple sentences to describe the main actions in each scene.

1. Some Catch

a. _____

b. _____

c. _____

d. _____

e. _____

2. Many Boons

a. _____

b. _____

c. _____

d. _____

e. _____

f. _____

g. _____

3. The Last Straw

a. _____

b. _____

c. _____

d. _____

III. CHARACTERS

List the main characters and write a few descriptive words for each.

_____

_____

_____

_____

_____

_____

IV. IMITATION

Rewrite "The Fisherman and His Wife"—first and second drafts.

- Be sure to include and underline all of the vocabulary words.

- Write three separate paragraphs, one for each scene (indent three times).

Bonus Challenge: Make the fish some other magical creature.

Story 20: Rapunzel

by the Brothers Grimm

1. Garden

There were once a man and a woman who had long in vain wished for a child. At length the woman hoped that God was about to grant her desire. These people had a little window at the back of their house from which a splendid garden could be seen, which was full of the most beautiful flowers and herbs. It was, however, surrounded by a high wall, and no one dared to go into it because it belonged to an enchantress who had great power and was dreaded by all the world. One day the woman was standing by this window and looking down into the garden, when she saw a bed which was planted with the most beautiful rampion (rapunzel). It looked so fresh and green that she longed for it and had the greatest desire to eat some. This desire increased every day, and as she knew that she could not get any of it, she pined away and began to look pale and miserable. Then her husband was alarmed and asked, "What ails you, dear wife?"

HISTORY

This story was told by Brothers Grimm, but began with "The Book of Kings," a long Persian poem written around AD 1000. It passed through Italy and France before reaching the Grimm brothers. It is a classic story about a witch having power over a princess and the prince needing to come to the rescue.

"Ah" she replied, "if I can't eat some of the rampion, which is in the garden behind our house, I shall die."

The man, who loved her, thought, "Sooner than let your wife die, bring her some of the rampion yourself, let it cost what it will."

At twilight, he clambered down over the wall into the garden of the enchantress, hastily clutched a handful of rampion, and took it to his wife. She at once made herself a salad of it and ate it greedily.

It tasted so good to her—so very good, that the next day she longed for it three times as much as before.

If he was to have any rest, her husband had to go down to the garden once again. In the gloom of evening, therefore, he let himself down again; but when he had clambered down the wall he was terribly afraid, for he saw the enchantress standing before him.

"How can you dare," said she with angry look, "to come down into my garden and steal my rampion like a thief? You shall suffer for it!"

"Ah," answered he, "let mercy take the place of justice, I only made up my mind to do it out of necessity. My wife saw your rampion from the window and felt such a longing for it that she would have died if she had not got some to eat."

Then the enchantress allowed her anger to be softened and said to him, "If things are as you say, I will allow you to take away with you as much rampion as you will, only I make one condition: you must give me the child which your wife will bring into the world. It shall be well treated, and I will care for it like a mother." The man in his terror consented to everything, and when the woman gave birth to a girl, the enchantress appeared at once, gave the child the name of Rapunzel, and took it away with her.

2. Tower

Rapunzel grew into the most beautiful child under the sun. When she was twelve years old, the enchantress shut her into a tower which lay in a forest and had neither stairs nor door, but quite at the top was a little window. When the enchantress wanted to go in, she placed herself beneath it and cried, "Rapunzel, Rapunzel, let down your hair to me."

Rapunzel had magnificent long hair, fine as spun gold. When she heard the voice of the enchantress, she unfastened her braided tresses, wound them round one of the hooks of the window above, and then the hair fell twenty ells down, and the enchantress climbed up by it.

After a year or two, it came to pass that the king's son rode through the forest and passed by the tower. Then he heard a song that was so charming that he stood still and listened. This was Rapunzel, who in her solitude passed her time by letting her sweet voice resound. The king's son wanted to climb up to her and looked for the door of the tower, but none was to be found. He rode home, but the singing had so deeply touched his heart, that every day he went out into the forest and listened to it. Once when he was thus standing behind a tree, he saw that an enchantress came there, and he heard how she cried, "Rapunzel, Rapunzel, let down your hair."

Then Rapunzel let down the braids of her hair, and the enchantress climbed up to her.

"If that is the ladder by which one mounts, I too will try my fortune," said he, and the next day when it began to grow dark, he went to the tower and cried, "Rapunzel, Rapunzel, let down your hair."

Immediately the hair fell down and the king's son climbed up.

At first Rapunzel was terribly frightened when a man, such as her eyes had never yet beheld, came to her, but the king's son began to talk to her like a friend and told her that his heart had been so stirred that it had let him have no rest, and he had been forced to see her. "I will willingly go away with you," she said, "but I do not know how to get down. Bring with you a skein of silk every time that you come, and I will weave a ladder with it, and when that is ready I will descend, and you will take me on your horse." They agreed that until that time he should come to her every evening, since the old woman came by day. The enchantress noticed nothing about this until once Rapunzel said to her, "Tell me, Dame Gothel, how it happens that you are so much heavier for me to draw up than the young king's son—he is with me in a moment?"

"Ah! you wicked child," cried the enchantress. "What do I hear you say! I thought I had separated you from all the world, and yet you have deceived me!"

In her anger she clutched Rapunzel's beautiful tresses, wrapped them twice round her left hand, seized a pair of scissors with the right, and snip, snap, they were cut off, and the lovely braids lay on the ground. And she was so pitiless that she took poor Rapunzel into a desert where she had to live in great grief and misery.

On the same day that she cast out Rapunzel, however, the enchantress fastened the braids of hair, which she had cut off, to the hook of the window, and when the king's son came and cried, "Rapunzel, Rapunzel, let down your hair," she let the hair down.

The king's son ascended, but instead of finding his dearest Rapunzel, he found the enchantress, who gazed at him with wicked and poisonous looks.

"Aha!" she cried mockingly, "you would fetch your dearest, but the beautiful bird sits no longer singing in the nest. The cat has got it and will scratch out your eyes as well. Rapunzel is lost to you. You will never see her again."

The king's son was beside himself with pain, and in his despair he leapt down from the tower. He escaped with his life, but the thorns into which he fell pierced his eyes. Then he wandered quite blind about the forest, ate nothing but roots and berries, and did nothing but lament and weep over the loss of his dearest Rapunzel.

3. Desert

Thus he roamed about in misery for some years and eventually came to the desert where Rapunzel lived in wretchedness. He heard a voice, and it seemed so familiar to him that he went toward it, and when he approached, Rapunzel knew him and fell on his neck and wept. Two of her tears wetted his eyes and they grew clear again, and he could see with them as before.

He led her to his kingdom, where he was joyfully received, and they lived for a long time afterward, happy and contented.

FINIS

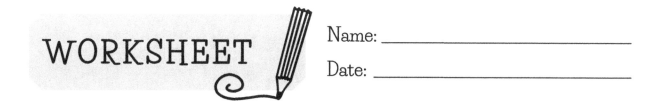

Name: _____

Date: _____

Story 20: Rapunzel

I. VOCABULARY

Underline the following words in the fable and define them below.

1. ails: _____

2. twilight: _____

3. clambered: _____

4. tresses: _____

5. ells: _____

6. solitude: _____

II. PLOT

Write simple sentences to describe the main actions in each scene.

1. Garden

a. _____

b. _____

c. _____

d. _____

e. _____

f. _____

2. Tower

a. _____

b. _____

c. _____

d. _____

e. _____

f. _____

g. _____

h. _____

i. _____

3. Desert

    a. _____

    b. _____

    c. _____

    d. _____

III. CHARACTERS

List the main characters and write a few descriptive words for each.

_____

_____

_____

_____

_____

_____

IV. IMITATION

Rewrite "Rapunzel"—first and second drafts.

- Be sure to include and underline all of the vocabulary words.

- Write three separate paragraphs, one for each scene (indent three times).

Bonus Challenge: Make something other than Rapunzel's hair the center of the story. Maybe Rapunzel has superpowers of some sort. Be creative.

Plot Key

Story 1: Why the Bear Has a Stumpy Tail

Slinking Along

a. Bear meets fox.

b. Fox has fish.

c. Bear asks advice.

Bad Advice

a. Fox tells lie.

b. Fish with tail.

c. In the ice.

d. Pull tail out.

A Strong Pull

a. Bear follows advice.

b. Bear's tail froze.

c. Bear pulled hard.

d. Tail snapped off.

e. Bruins lack tails.

Story 2: The Princess and the Pea

The Search

a. Prince wants princess.

b. Prince travels far.

c. Prince finds none.

d. Prince returns home.

The Test

a. Real princess arrives.

b. Queen places pea.

c. Queen covers pea.

d. Princess lays down.

The Outcome

a. Princess sleeps poorly.

b. Princess is sensitive.

c. Princess is real.

d. Prince marries princess.

e. Museum holds pea.

Story 3: The Fox and the Horse

Turned Adrift

a. Farmer has horse.

b. Horse grows old.

c. Return when stronger.

d. Horse turned adrift.

e. Horse sought shelter.

f. Horse meets fox.

The Plan

a. Fox makes plan.

b. Horse lies down.

c. Fox gets lion.

d. Fox tricks lion.

Hog-Tied

a. Lion lies down.

b. Fox ties knot.

c. Horse drags lion.

d. Horse returns home.

e. Farmer's heart relented.

f. Horse lived happily.

Story 4: Ali and the Sultan's Saddle

Ali's Jokes

a. Ali ridicules Sultan.

b. Folk enjoy mockery.

c. Word reaches Sultan.

d. Sultan summons Ali.

Before the Sultan

a. Forehead scraped floor.

b. Ali praises Sultan.

c. Ali invents poem.

d. Splendor like sun.

e. Strength like tempest.

f. Voice like wind.

g. All people cheer.

h. Sultan is charmed.

Ali's Reward

a. Sultan praises Ali.

b. Sultan gives saddle.

c. Saddle on back.

d. People question Ali.

e. I honored Sultan.

f. Sultan gave robe.

g. Winking, Ali pointed

Story 5: The Straw, the Coal, and the Bean

Great Escape

a. Woman cooks beans.

b. Woman burns straw.

c. Out jumps bean.

d. Out jumps coal.

e. Three become friends.

Joined in Fellowship

a. Bean makes proposal.

b. Friends begin travels.

c. Friends encounter brook.

Black Seam

a. Straw becomes bridge.

b. Coal trots out.

c. Coal becomes petrified.

d. Coal burns straw.

e. Bean bursts laughing.

f. Tailor repairs bean.

g. Beans have seams.

Story 6: The Three Billy Goats Gruff

Greener Grass

a. Goats named Gruff.

b. Want to cross bridge.

c. Troll under bridge.

d. Eyes like saucers.

e. Nose like poker.

Two Across

a. Smallest goat crosses.

b. Smallest meets troll.

c. Troll allows passage.

d. Middle goat crosses.

e. Middle meets troll.

f. Troll allows passage.

Butted Off

a. Big goat crosses.

b. Biggest meets troll.

c. Biggest butts troll.

d. Brothers become fat.

Story 7: The Pied Piper of Hamelin

Rats in Hamelin

a. Hamelin has rats.

b. Rats spoiled beauty.

c. Mayor is responsible.

Strange Piper

a. Queer piper enters.

b. Piper can charm.

c. Mayor gives word.

d. Piper plays tune.

e. Rats are drowned.

A Different Tune

a. Piper wants guilders.

b. Mayor breaks promise.

c. Piper plays tune.

d. Children led away.

e. Town was lonesome.

Story 8: The Queen Bee

Mercy Shown

a. Sons seek fortune.

b. Dwarf seeks brothers.

c. Youngest spares ants.

d. Youngest spares ducks.

e. Youngest spares bees.

1,000 Pearls

a. Brothers find castle.

b. Man feeds brothers.

c. Eldest seeks pearls.

d. Eldest becomes stone.

e. Second seeks pearls.

f. Second becomes stone.

g. Brothers marry princesses.

The Disenchantment

a. Dwarf seeks pearls.

b. Dwarf begins crying.

c. Ants find pearls.

d. Ducks find key.

e. Bee chooses youngest.

f. Spell is broken.

Story 9: Old Sultan

Useless

a. Shepherd's faithful dog.

b. Old and toothless.

c. I'll shoot Sultan.

d. Wife says no.

e. Tomorrow he dies.

The Rescue

a. Sultan seeks advice.

b. Wolf makes plan.

c. Sultan rescues child.

d. Shepherd changes mind.

One Good Turn. . .

a. Wolf wants sheep.

b. Sultan tells shepherd.

c. Shepherd cudgels wolf.

d. Boar challenges Sultan.

e. Sultan brings cat.

f. Cat scares enemy.

g. Wolf promises friendship.

Story 10: The Mouse, the Bird, and the Sausage

Fowl Discontent

a. Partnership is entered.

b. Friends greatly prosper.

c. Bird gathered wood.

d. Mouse fetched water.

e. Sausage did cooking.

f. Bird was mocked.

g. Bird became discontent.

Content Canine

a. Bird wanted change.

b. Friends drew lots.

c. Sausage gathered wood.

d. Mouse did cooking.

e. Bird fetched water.

f. Dog ate sausage.

g. Bird found out.

Making the Best of It

a. Friends fix meal.

b. Mouse jumps in.

c. Mouse lost life.

d. House catches fire.

e. Bird falls in well.

f. Bird is drowned.

Story 11: The Elves and the Cobbler

Mysterious Help

a. Cobbler works hard.

b. Cobbler cuts leather.

c. Poor cobbler sleeps.

d. Shoes are made.

e. Customer buys shoes.

f. Cobbler buys leather.

g. Shoes are made.

The Discovery

a. Couple watches quietly.

b. In come elves.

c. Elves make shoes.

d. Wife proposes plan.

e. Clothes are made.

f. Clothes are left.

g. Couple watches again.

Highly Delighted

a. Elves are delighted.

b. Elves get dressed.

c. Elves dance away.

d. Couple lives happily.

Story 12: The Wolf and the Seven Little Kids

Home Alone

a. Goat loves kids.

b. Goat prepared kids.

c. Don't worry mom.

d. Goat entered forest.

Wolf at the Door

a. Wolf wants in.

b. Kids recognize voice.

c. Wolf eats chalk.

d. Kids recognize paws.

e. Wolf whitens feet.

f. Kids open door.

g. Wolf eats kids.

h. Wolf falls asleep.

Mother Returns

a. Mother comes home.

b. Youngest tells story.

c. Mother opens wolf.

d. Kids spring out.

e. Stones put in.

f. Mother sews wolf.

g. Wolf wants water.

h. Wolf drowns miserably.

Story 13: The Three Children of Fortune

The Inheritance

a. Father gives gifts.

b. Oldest receives cock.

c. Second receives scythe.

d. Youngest receives cat.

e. Rarity=great value.

Rare Value

a. Old father dies.

b. Oldest seeks demand.

c. Natives pay gold.

d. Second seeks demand.

e. People pay gold.

f. Youngest seeks demand.

g. He earns double.

The Cost of Ignorance

a. Cat eats mice.

b. Cat meows thirstily.

c. King is afraid.

d. Herald warns cat.

e. King attacks castle.

f. Cat runs away.

g. Palace is leveled.

Story 14: The Frog Prince

Promise Made

a. Princess lost ball.

b. Frog makes deal.

c. Princess promises friendship.

d. Frog retrieves ball.

e. Princess breaks promise.

Promise Kept

a. Frog comes calling.

b. Princess slams door.

c. King learns story.

d. Perform your promise.

e. Princess "befriends" frog.

Charm Broken

a. Frog becomes prince.

b. Prince tells story.

c. Prince proposes marriage.

d. King gives consent.

e. Couple live happily.

Story 15: The Golden Goose

Three Sons

a. Man with sons.

b. Oldest cuts wood.

c. Meets old man.

d. Man causes mischief.

e. Second does same.

f. Dummling shares provisions.

g. Man gives blessing.

Golden Goose

a. Dummling finds goose.

b. Stays at inn.

c. Sisters stick fast.

d. Parson sticks fast.

e. Clerk sticks fast.

f. Laborers stick fast.

g. Seven follow Dummling.

Traveling Train

a. Dummling travels on.

b. Train enters city.

c. Princess won't laugh.

d. King makes promise.

e. Train causes laughter.

f. Dummling marries princess.

Story 16: The Man in the Bag

Prince of Turnips

a. Brothers are soldiers.

b. Poorest sowed turnips.

c. Huge turnip harvested.

d. King receives turnip.

e. King blesses poorest.

A Brother's Envy

a. Richest envies brother.

b. Richest gives gift.

c. King gives turnip.

d. Richest plots murder.

e. Villains are interrupted.

f. Brother left hanging.

Sack of Wisdom

a. Brother makes hole.

b. Student rides up.

c. Brother praises bag.

d. Student trades places.

e. Brother rides home.

f. Student learns wisdom.

Story 17: The Emperor's New Clothes

Excessively Fond

a. Emperor loves clothes.

b. Two rogues come.

c. Rogues could weave.

d. Invisible if unfit.

e. Invisible if stupid.

f. Emperor gives cash.

g. Rogues begin "weaving."

Loom Lunacy

a. Emperor is curious.

b. Emperor sends minister.

c. Minister sees nothing.

d. Minister says differently.

e. Emperor views clothes.

f. Emperor sees nothing.

g. Emperor says differently.

Words of the Innocent

a. Rogues "work" hard.

b. Rogues "dress" Emperor.

c. Emperor admires himself.

d. Emperor begins procession.

e. People praise clothes.

f. Child speaks truth.

g. Emperor proceeds.

Story 18: King Grizzle-Beard

Ill-Treatment

a. Princess is proud.

b. Suitors brought forward.

c. Princess makes sport.

d. King makes vow.

Hard Lessons

a. Traveling fiddler comes.

b. Princess marries fiddler.

c. Princess regrets spitefulness.

d. Princess tries weaving.

e. Princess tries spinning.

f. Princess tries earthenware.

g. Princess becomes maid.

Marriage Feast

a. Princess bitterly grieved.

b. King wants dance.

c. Princess receives jeering.

d. Princess tries escape.

e. King reveals plan.

f. Princess has wisdom.

g. Feast takes place.

Story 19: The Fisherman and his Wife

Some Catch

a. Couple in pigsty.

b. Fisherman catches fish.

c. Fish begs mercy.

d. Fisherman releases fish.

e. Wife commands husband.

Many Boons

a. Fisherman calls fish.

b. Fisherman requests cottage.

c. Wife is discontent.

d. Fisherman requests castle.

e. Wife is discontent.

f. Fisherman requests kingship.

g. Wife is discontent.

The Last Straw

a. Fisherman calls fish.

b. Fisherman requests Lordship.

c. Fisherman lost all.

d. Couple return impoverished.

Story 20: Rapunzel

Garden

a. Parents want child.

b. Woman desires rampion.

c. Man steals rampion.

d. Enchantress catches man.

e. Man promises child.

f. Enchantress takes Rapunzel.

Tower

a. Enchantress climbs hair.

b. Prince hears voice.

c. Prince sees enchantress.

d. Prince climbs hair.

e. Rapunzel tells enchantress.

f. Enchantress cuts hair.

g. Enchantress takes Rapunzel.

h. Enchantress catches Prince.

i. Prince is blinded.

Desert

a. Prince hears voice.

b. Prince finds Rapunzel.

c. Tears cure sight.

FINIS

Made in the USA
Monee, IL
09 October 2024

66988958R00096